Believe

A Tale of Faye

Allyson L. Giles

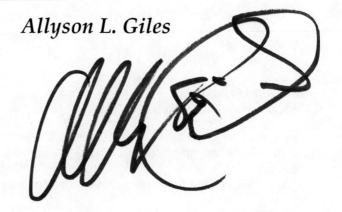

Strategic Book Group

Strategic Book Group
P.O. Box 333
Durham CT 06422
www.StrategicBookGroup.com

ISBN: 978-1-60911-898-3

Book Design: Rolando F. Santos

For all of you out there who dare to believe…
this is for you.

With love,
Ally

Acknowledgments

Heartfelt gratitude and thanks to my editor and agent Keren Kilgore. I will be forever grateful for having found you. Thank you for your guidance and support; you made me and this book better. Thank you to Carolyn Ferris for connecting me with Keren. Thanks also to Dee Berryhill for helping me discover my passion for writing. Thank you to Steve, my brother and illustrator, for believing in my dream of Faye long before it became a reality. Thanks to my family and friends for your support and inspiration. Many thanks to everyone at Strategic Book Group. I appreciate your decision to give me and my story a chance. Most of all, I thank Strategic for making this journey an enjoyable one. And, of course, mad love to all my elemental friends and guides for allowing me to share in your magical world.

Glossary of Important Terms

Elementals, Nature spirits: Nature spirits, which include fairies or elementals, are believed to be various types of beings or spirits that inhabit nature. Nature spirits usually abide in trees, rivers, plants, mountains, and minerals. They are believed to exist as the life force in all living things.

Blueprint: A detailed outline or plan of action.

Prophecy: The foretelling or prediction of what is to come; something that is declared by a prophet, especially a divinely inspired prediction, instruction, or exhortation.

Long ago in a faraway land…
A baby was delivered, a prophecy planned.
The girl unaware of the journey she would take,
Of the love and the light she would spread for a realm's sake.
One child's prophecy and a kingdom come undone.
Half-human, half-elemental the blueprint did state.
The time was upon them; the girl had grown
And one by one they would appear and lead her home….

Chapter 1

And the fairies jump and dance and play.
Deep in the grass and bushes and trees,
Fairies will do as they please.
They are in touch with the beauty of land.
The soil beneath your feet is nothing more than a fairy treat.

Hearing a loud knock, Sam opened the creaky front door of the cottage he called home and froze in shock. It was unusual for a visitor to make his way this far out in the Irish countryside without notice, but Sam was a spontaneous fellow and enjoyed surprises. Little did he know that he was opening the door to the biggest surprise of his life: a basket containing a teeny, tiny, smiling, giggling baby with wide eyes that looked up at him from beneath a blanket and bonnet of pink wool. A large pink ribbon was tied to the basket with a note sealed by purple wax. Sam's name was handwritten in calligraphy on the front of the note. On instinct, Sam picked up the basket, took the baby inside, and sat down by the fire. Before anxiously opening the envelope, he noted the *F* marked in the wax seal. He read the note aloud:

A riddle, a riddle, a riddle you say.
Perhaps you weren't expecting baby.
A rhyme, a rhyme, a rhyme it is.
This child is yours and ours to live.
You are not alone, but keep her you must;
All I can say is in Faye you must trust.
A father, a father, a father you are—
A man who will father the blueprint and star.

3

Sam looked down and saw several tiny, winged beings sitting around the basket. They were oooing and aaawing over the child. Sam shook his head in complete confusion. Without another word, Sam got up and made himself a cup of hot cider in the kitchen, hoping that the hallucination would pass. He sipped the hot drink before making his way back to his favorite fireside chair. Rubbing his eyes, he then turned toward the basket and opened them quickly.

"What in heaven's name? Fairies? They are still here, but now there are seven!"

Their silver, gold, and rainbow-colored wings sparkled like the wings of a dragonfly, and the fairies were remarkably small with pointy ears. Some even had pointy feet. Some were bright in color, others were translucent, and some just seemed to glow. Still fixated on the tiny beings surrounding the mysterious baby, Sam tossed back his cider.

The fairies began to whisper to one another in a high-pitched buzz with tiny squeaks every once in awhile. Then one fairy draped in a long, green, velvet gown with gold embellishments and long, curly, blonde hair stepped forward from the group.

"I am Elvina," she said in a soft, soothing voice. "I am the child's spirit guide. I will help you raise her, Sam. I will always be with her and will help and serve her in every way."

"I'm sorry. Did you just talk?" Sam knew what his eyes were seeing and what his ears were hearing, but his mind couldn't grasp it. "This just isn't possible or logical or...."

"Sam," Elvina chimed in, "don't listen to your mind. Listen to your heart. You have had one wish your entire life: to love and to experience true love in return. Until today, this wish has been unfulfilled. This is your purpose, Sam: to be open to the love you have wanted for so long. We are not a figment of your imagination; we are very real indeed, and we live among you, right outside your back door and in your home. We are—and always have been—everywhere. We tend to your animals and plants, work with Mother Nature, and help humans like you who have a deep connection to the land. This child is half-human and half-elemental, meaning she is one of us. She is half-fairy."

Sam raised an eyebrow, perplexed. He had always been in touch with nature, and there was nothing he enjoyed more than being a fisherman and spending time out on the boat at peace with the wind and the water. He suddenly remembered an experience he'd had as a child and gasped. He had thought he'd seen a fairy hovering above a bluebell one day. In his innocence, he eagerly told his parents and friends, but they laughed at him and endlessly teased him. After that, he didn't believe, and he never saw one again. Until today.

A male fairy came forward dressed in a brown cap; a blazer; shorts that revealed a slim, beige body; and brown, pointy-toed shoes. He looked very much like a newsboy. His wings were buzzing, and he looked rather excited.

"I'm Tatum! The fairy you saw as a child, 'twas me. I did try to come back to ya, but you were never open to me again after that. 'Twas a shame," he said sadly as he removed the cap from his head and bowed slightly. "Happens all the time. It's funny; a human can tell you something bad, and wham bang you believe it. When they tell you something good—like seeing a fairy—they think you're crazy!"

Tatum and the fairies started to laugh loudly. Then he placed his brown cap back on his head and kicked up his pointy-toed foot on the edge of the baby's wicker basket, and the little winged beings started to dance around it. Even the baby watched happily and waved her hands in the air every so often as if to join in. Sam had no idea where the music came from, but it was suddenly there and unmistakable. It was like Irish folk music, and it didn't take long for the fairies to kick up their heels and make themselves at home.

The night wore on in celebration, as did the ensuing months and years with daily visits from the fairies.

• • •

Sam continued picking dandelions for Deliah. She danced and spun in the grass as he wove them together, making her one of his famous dandelion crowns. He placed it on her head and declared her a true princess.

"You have a gift, my dear. A bright light shines in you, and you will be someone and mean something to this world. You bring out the best in people and make them want to believe in the good. People would follow you, Deliah, wherever you would lead them," Papa acknowledged.

5

She curtsied, enjoying every moment of make-believe and then began running to the riverbank.

"Come on, Papa! Let's skip rocks."

Sam jogged behind her, and after arriving at the riverbank, they began searching for the perfect flat rocks. Having found several handfuls, they stepped on to the worn dock and began skipping them, taking extra care not to skip them in the direction of Papa's fishing boat. When they were done skipping all the flat rocks they could find, they headed back to the cottage to have a picnic. After making their favorite peanut butter and jelly sandwiches, they went back outside and sat in the middle of the grass, enjoying their picnic in the warm afternoon sun. They continued to tell each other stories, always trying to be more creative than the other. When their picnic was finished, they decided to pick blueberries and raspberries from the bushes behind the cottage. They both relished in their love of nature and enjoyed any time spent outdoors among the flowers, trees, and animals. Often, Deliah would find a stray cat or a wounded bird and bring it home. She and Papa would heal these animals with secret help from the fairies and then set them free. Sam always admired Deliah's caring nature; even at the age of ten, she was already giving back to the world in her own special way.

When it got dark, they would have bonfires and roast marshmallows, and Papa would tell make-believe stories about fairies while they stared at the stars. It was a special treat when they managed to glimpse a shooting star. Sam and Deliah always liked the same things, so it was never a struggle to have fun or entertain each other.

• • •

Sam became very close to his numerous fairy friends, and he felt privileged being in on the world's best-kept secret. But along with Deliah, his little girl who appeared on his doorstep that fateful night, the fairies were his family, and they gave him the best memories of his life. Whenever he felt he didn't know how to handle a situation or wondered if he was raising Deliah properly, Elvina remained true to her word. She was always there to guide Sam and assure him that he was doing just fine. Although she made him promise to never tell Deliah that she was born of a different realm (the fairy realm) and that she was part-elemental and part-human, Elvina's words would echo over and over in his mind: *She will know, Sam. Do not fear. When the time is right, she will see us here.*

Sam knew that Deliah was part of a bigger plan and that she would find out on her own when the time was right. He also knew she would have the opportunity to serve the fairies and Mother Nature. He couldn't wait until Deliah was old enough to know all about the fairies. He never told anyone—not even his mother, even though she helped him raise the baby girl without even asking a question about her mysterious appearance.

• • •

The rain fell hard, and the lightning crashed. It was the worst storm Sam had seen in years. He was trying to get back home to Deliah to celebrate her eleventh birthday, but this storm was raging a fierce fight. He held on to the boat's wheel, first spinning it hard right, then hard left, trying to keep her steady. He held on tight as *Little Lady*, his pride and joy, rocked back and forth, waves crashing down on her from every angle. Sam remained grounded and focused despite the chaos whirling around him. He had grown up fishing, observing, and learning from his father, the fisherman he most admired. He knew not to let his nerves get the best of him; it was about remaining calm and working with the water, not against it. Sam began talking to the storm as he often did. It was a trick his father had taught him when he was a wee lad.

Raising his voice, he shouted out into the dangerous downpour, "Come on now! Ya know I've got a little lady to get home to. You wouldn't keep me from my daughter's birthday, would ya?" Another bolt of lightning clapped in the air, causing him to jump.

He chuckled and said, "All right, all right, you're not in the mood for a chitchat, I gather."

One of the sails came undone and began flapping furiously in the wind. The boat was losing control, and Sam hung on to the wheel with his right hand while reaching far behind him with his left for the tail end of the rope. His feet slid, and he lost hold of the wheel but quickly managed to tie the sail back down. He was trying to get back to the helm, but his galoshes were heavy and had no grip against the soaked floor of the boat. The boat

7

continued to sway, and when it began to tilt forward, he stepped out and was just about to take hold of the wheel when he saw it....A large tidal wave was about to come crashing down on top of *Little Lady*. Looking in horror, he tried to brace himself, but the wave caught him first, and he was thrown. The back of his head hit the wheel hard.

"Deliah," he mumbled as his world faded to black.

• • •

"Where's Papa? He should have been here an hour ago," Deliah asked for the seventh time in ten minutes.

"He'll be back, Deliah. The storm is just holding him up awhile. Don't you worry. He'll be home soon, my dear," Grandma replied, trying to mask the concern in her own voice.

"Well, let's go wait for him on the dock," Deliah urged.

"Deliah, your father would not want you out in this storm. He'd want you to stay put, safe and sound," she said with authority. Deliah picked up her and Papa's favorite book and stomped off to her room. "Where are you going, Deliah? Would you like me to read your book to you?"

"No," Deliah answered curtly, slamming the door slightly for extra effect. She sat on her bed pouting when she decided that if Grandma wouldn't take her to the dock to wait for Papa, then she would just have to go herself. She crept quietly out of her bedroom and snuck down the hall past the living room, where her Grandma sat sipping tea and staring into the fire. As quietly as she could, Deliah made her way to the back door. On her tiptoes, she managed to pull down her raincoat and hat from their hook. She slowly slid out the back door, feeling proud to have made it outside unnoticed.

Outside, she was taken back by the scary storm. Nevertheless, she ran as fast as her legs would allow to the dock to see if she could see Papa's boat coming in. She could almost hear Papa whisper "Happy birthday, little lady" as she imagined him running up the riverbank to greet her. She stood, getting pounded by the rain, searching the dark sky for....

"Papa!" she shrieked. She saw the boat not far from the dock; it was tipped over and bobbing slightly on its side. Deliah felt sick but ran to the end of the dock.

"Papa!" she screamed over and over toward the boat, her voice a mere whisper in the wild wind. It was foggy and dark except for a couple lights on the dock.

"Papa! Papa!" she screamed, clinging to the end of the dock.

On her knees, she scanned the water with her eyes. She cried in horror as she saw something float by. It was Papa's raincoat…. It was….

She stood, turned, and took off running. She slammed into her grandmother, who appeared right behind her. Grandma took one look at the body in the water and hugged Deliah so tightly that Deliah thought she might break. She couldn't tell if it was tears or the rain streaming down Grandma's face. Deliah wiggled loose. Gripping the dock tightly, she reached out for Papa.

"Hurry! We have to help! Hurry!" she cried hysterically, but Grandma knew they were too late.

They both waded into the cold water, grabbed Papa's raincoat, and pulled him to shore. Deliah couldn't bear her loss. Heaving with sobs, she fell on top of Papa. After a few minutes, Grandma knew that they needed to get help and that Deliah couldn't stay out in the rain. She picked up Deliah and carried her kicking and screaming back to the cottage, knowing their lives would never be the same.

It was a sad day for the elementals when Sam suddenly passed away, but they knew Deliah would be all right. In true fairy fashion, they didn't mourn but celebrated his life. And Deliah's grandmother loved her as though she were her own, so Deliah was in good hands. Although the fairies were with Deliah since her arrival on earth, they couldn't reveal themselves to her until she was old enough to trust them. Deliah was born for an important purpose in life, and she had to be handled delicately. If the fairies were to reveal themselves and the prophecy to her too soon, the prophecy could fail, so they waited for the eleventh day of the eleventh month of her eleventh year. To the fairies, this represented a time of open doors, magic, and opportunity.

Deliah
Ostephen Kristoff

Chapter 2

Run through the grass with reckless abandon.
Let down your hair in true fairy fashion.
We live for the joy, the games, and the laughter,
For, you see, these are your keys to happily ever after.

As she sat in the tall grass of the meadow, feeling the grass tickle her skin and watching the breeze drift through the trees causing the leaves to fall, Deliah realized that life would never be the same. The serenity and calm she always felt in the presence of nature had all but ceased to exist. Her cheeks flushed red as her body tightened with anger.

Not again, she thought as her body gave way to yet another fit of tears and despair.

"I am so sick of this!" she wept. "I'm sick of crying and feeling angry and sad all the time! Why...?" she cried. "He was so kind and good. And he loved me." Feeling heartsick, she sobbed.

"You could have taken anyone! Why Papa?" Why?"

She was almost twelve, and the question had been haunting her for several months now. Her world was shaken to the core, and she was losing the battle for her faith.

She had always been a very creative, happy child, and just being around her brought a smile to anyone's face. She remembered Papa telling her that she was beautiful and different, that she had a gift and a bright light about her, but she didn't feel like that now. Deliah, you see, had a characteristically different look to her. Her ears were a tad pointy, and her nose was a tad pointy, too. Her long brown hair cascaded over her shoulders in

11

ethereal form. Her cheeks permanently flushed a glowing pink. Her lips were stained a fine shade of raspberry, and her eyes were big and expressive. She was a very small girl, but her heart was huge—and at the moment, broken.

Deliah slowly lifted her head from her knees. Through her tear-stained, blurry gaze, she seemed to spot something. Wiping away her tears on the long sleeve of her white cotton dress, she tried to focus. Suddenly her gaze shifted to a flicker in the grass a few yards away. She was drawn toward what seemed to be a tiny glowing light. The light started to move as if it were swimming through the luscious, green blades of grass. As she followed it, she was consumed by the beauty and the love it was giving off. Deliah sat very still, careful not to make a noise as the light stopped a few yards away from her at the top of a tiny embankment.

What is that? she wondered as a faint noise came from the area. The noise began to get louder, and Deliah thought she heard a singsong or some kind of rhyming chant.

"Well, hello! We've been expectin' ya," she heard. Deliah looked around but didn't see anyone. "Down here, me dear, by the light."

The light began to get bigger and brighter, causing everything around it to sparkle and glow. She crouched down in the grass, and using her hand to shield her eyes, she peered past the still-expanding, glorious white light and saw a tiny wooden door. Just as she reached for it, it burst open, and a flitter of fairies came pouring out, holding hands and singing loudly, "Fairy fun and fairy games as we dance among the fairy flames! Smiles and laughter, joy and glee! Come and join the fairy family!"

Deliah was captivated and stared silently with her big brown eyes as wide as saucers. She wondered if the make-believe stories Papa used to tell her really were true. Before Deliah knew it, the fairies had crowded around her, and she was in a circle, holding hands and singing along. She was grinning from ear to ear with not a care in the world. For the first time in a long time, Deliah was happy and felt like a kid again. After much singing and dancing, she plopped down on the grass and giggled endlessly with her newfound friends.

"We knew you'd be findin' us soon, dear. I'm Mayweather!" an older-looking fairy exclaimed.

"Nice to meet you, but I should get back before my grandmother starts to worry," Deliah said, suddenly realizing how long she'd been gone.

"No need to fret, me dear," Mayweather replied. "We can stop time for you if we need to; it'll yield when necessary. Your grandmother won't even blink; she's sleepin' soundly by the fire."

"I don't understand," Deliah said. "Why would it be necessary to stop time for me? I'm nothing special."

Astonished at her remark, the fairies grew silent.

"Nothin' special!" Mayweather gasped, holding onto the ribbons of her floral bonnet as if it were about to jump off her head. With wide eyes, the other fairies leaned in close, gripping her with their intent stares.

"Deliah, it's time we told you why you stumbled upon us today," Mayweather declared. "'Tis no accident, little lady. You have a destiny to help save our kingdom. Your Papa knew this." The fairies' wings wilted, and their eyes shrunk with sadness as they all sighed heavily and sunk down into the grass.

"The Dark Ones are taking over our land," Mayweather continued. "One by one, they are turning the good fairies to their side, and we need your help to save the kingdom, or all of Faye will be forever lost."

"But why me? What can I possibly do, and when did you see Papa?" She abruptly hopped to her feet. Suddenly angry again, she asked, "Is this some kind of mean joke?"

Deliah felt a gentle pull on the hem of her dress. A little blue fairy in a tiny, timid voice drenched in sincerity said, "'Tis no joke, Deliah. They took my brother. Kristoff was pure of heart but easily tempted, and they caught him...." His blue eyes swelled up with tears, and he coughed to clear his throat.

Deliah knelt down in the grass and looked into his eyes. "I'm terribly sorry about your brother; I know how it feels to lose someone."

The blue fairy reached out his right hand and introduced himself, "I'm Ostephen."

Deliah, afraid to shake his tiny hand for fear she may hurt him, laid her palm in the grass for Ostephen to climb on. She raised her left hand to eye level and said, "Pleased to meet you,

Ostephen." After a moment's silence, Deliah looked around at all the fairies' intent and worried faces and asked, "Can I see my father? Is he here?"

"He's on a different plane, dear, but he is with you. He never really left. He watches over you day and night; he's become your guardian angel."

Deliah, even more confused, sighed heavily.

"Cordelia has asked to see you," Mayweather interrupted. "I don't mean to rush you, me dear, but when Cordelia asks for your attendance, 'tis an honor to be bestowed. She's the keeper of the flowers of Faye. She makes flowers bloom and gardens grow. Without her, there'd be neither summer nor spring. Perhaps you could just trust in us a wee bit and listen to what Cordelia has to say? If you don't like what she has to offer, by all means, we'll leave ya be. I promise."

Ostephen, still sitting comfortably in her palm, looked deep into her eyes and with pleading desperation said, "We can't do it without ya. 'Tis the blueprint. Half-elemental, half-human that's the leader, the savior."

"I'm not half-anything," Deliah said, trying to be understanding. "I'm just me."

"Cordelia can explain," Ostephen said.

Utterly perplexed, Deliah realized that there was only one way she'd get answers, and whether it was her innate sense of adventure or that strange rumbling in her gut, something inside urged her to follow them.

With her hands on her hips, she declared, "Well, let's go. We don't want to keep Cordelia waiting."

The fairies cheered excitedly. With their little wings buzzing and flapping wildly, they jumped in the air.

"This way, Dearie," Mayweather's white-gloved hand waved her on.

Ostephen, overjoyed with her decision, stuttered as he tried to find the right words, and Deliah giggled.

"I know, I know," she said and playfully dropped him into her front pocket.

Climbing up to the edge of her pocket with a shiny, silver-wrapped chocolate candy in his hand, Ostephen proclaimed, "Deliah, silver and chocolate! This is the perfect gift for

14

Cordelia!"

Deliah laughed and said, "I always keep a few in my pocket."

"You are more fairy than you realize," Ostephen muttered under his breath. "Got anymore in there?" he asked as he peered down.

A little confused as to what he meant, she replied, "No, that was my last one. I ate the others."

"Fine. We'll save it for Cordelia," he said defeated, dropping the candy back into her pocket. Flying up and taking a seat on her shoulder, he began to sing, "Fairy fun and fairy games as we dance among the fairy flames…."

Mermaid

Chapter 3

Open your eyes, and you will see
Just what you've been missing
If only you'd believed.

A short while later, they arrived at the foot of a great oak tree, and the fairies all knocked in sync on the bark—rap, rap, rap—three times. A tiny door carved in the bark opened, and a little silver fairy peered out.

"We are here to honor Cordelia's request for our attendance. We have the blueprint," said Mayweather, enthusiastically pointing to the child. The bark door closed, and the fairy disappeared only to reemerge seconds later.

"Cordelia is pleased to honor your attendance and will meet you in the flowers of Faye garden," he said, pointing to his left. They all nodded and bowed as he closed the door and disappeared once more.

The glowing garden was filled with an abundance of wildflowers: bright marigold, lavender, pansy, shamrock, tulip, and lily. There were more flowers than Deliah could ever begin to name, all growing wild and free.

Papa would have loved this, she thought.

The fairies took their seats. Some sat on bluebells, some on foxgloves, others on tiny twigs and leaves. Deliah picked a spot where she wouldn't hurt any flowers and leaned against the base of a pine tree.

"This garden is amazing!" Deliah said, glancing about.

She heard a regal voice say, "Thank you."

Deliah turned to see a fairy dressed in a long gown of deep red with silver lining and bell sleeves walking toward her. A crown of silver bells adorned the fairy's honey-colored hair.

Before Deliah had a chance to get up, Cordelia knelt before her and said, "It is an honor to meet you. Thank you for coming." After rising to her silver-slippered feet, the fairy continued, "Faye is in danger. There are Dark Ones who are slowly turning the good fairies bad and taking over our land. It is written in the blueprints, the prophecy of Faye, that a time will come when the land will be rescued by a child, a girl who is half-human and half-elemental. You, dear Deliah, are that child."

Deliah was about to interrupt and correct this poor, mistaken fairy when Cordelia hurriedly cut in.

"Deliah, you are a part of us. You are half-fairy, half-human. Your pointy ears and pointier nose are a few of the characteristics you've been unable to hide."

Deliah touched her ears, then slid her hand to her nose. She'd never thought about it before, but, come to think of it, Grandma didn't have pointy ears, and neither did Papa.

Actually, she'd asked Papa once, and he had replied, "You are the most beautiful girl I've ever seen. Don't ever let anyone tell you differently, you understand."

She smiled, thinking of Papa. Then she remembered that she wasn't alone.

"Cordelia, I just don't know that I'm who you think I am or that I'm able to do anything to help."

"I understand your fears, Deliah, and all I can ask is that you trust in us, trust in Faye."

All the fairies were anxiously perched on the edges of their seats, hands clasped, wings still, praying that Deliah wouldn't leave them hopeless.

Deliah looked from Ostephen's face to Mayweather's, and then back to Cordelia's. Deliah shrugged her shoulders and took a deep breath. Everything had fallen so quiet that she swore she heard Papa's voice whisper in her ears, "Do not worry. Do not fear. They won't lead you astray, and I'll always be here. Remember when I told you that you would make your mark. Well, here, my sweet child, is where you must start."

Deliah felt her heart swell and then taking another deep

breath, she slowly reached into her pocket and pulled out the silver-wrapped chocolate. The fairies buzzed with excitement! They had a penchant for shiny, silver things as well as chocolate, so this was quite a gift! She laid it before Cordelia who bowed graciously.

"Okay, I'm in," Deliah said.

Instantaneously, Irish folk music rose up, and the fairies jumped up and started celebrating. They all crowded around Deliah, glowing brightly. They hugged her, some around the ankle, some the arm, and some even bounced atop her head to joyfully spread their thanks.

The silver fairy came out from behind the bark door with a large silver bell, and using it as a megaphone, Cordelia shouted, "The blueprint has accepted!"

Deliah laughed and walked with Cordelia back to her oak tree before joining the other fairies for the party. They drank from honeysuckles, rode on white fairy horses, and danced and sang the night away.

The next morning, Deliah awoke in the garden. She expected it to all be a wild dream, but she felt a little blue fairy tugging at the sleeve of her dress and pointing to a plate of fruit, cookies, and milk.

"Thought you might be hungry," he said.

"Thanks, Ostephen," Deliah said hesitantly, coming to terms with the fact that this wasn't at all a dream.

"Don't worry about your grandmother," he said. "We sent Tatum to stay with her and make sure she's protected. No harm can come her way. She'll wake up eventually and won't remember a thing; she'll feel like she had the best sleep of her life."

Deliah's stomach started to grumble, so she reached for a cookie and took a sip of the milk. She noticed it was regular human food and asked Ostephen how they managed to get it.

"Oh, we have plenty of human friends who leave us treats all the time in exchange for us helping their gardens grow or healing their animals. Plus, not to brag, but fairies are known for their manifestation skills; all we need to do is think of what we need, and—poof!—we can have it."

Deliah nodded in surprise. "Did the fairies help heal all the animals I brought home to Papa?"

"Of course!" Ostephen said, feeling pleased with her discovery.

She looked around and saw that a few fairies were still sleeping in the garden. It looked like something out of a fairy tale that Papa used to read her, and she giggled. There were fairies curled up, sleeping inside bluebells and hanging over foxgloves; others made a hanging shelter out of broad leaves. But Deliah's favorite thing was that some of the fairies wore nightcaps and slippers made of leaves with little dandelion balls on the end. She smiled when she realized how glad she was to have discovered this magical world and how she didn't feel completely sad for the first time in so long.

A short while later, the fairies gathered and explained to Deliah just how the Dark Ones were ruining their land and leading their people, creatures, and beauty astray.

"They tempt them, you see. They can sense what it is you most desire or yearn for (always the most materialistic and selfish thing), and then they find a way to make you believe it's yours. Before you realize it's a trick, it's too late, and the soul of the fairy is held captive by the Dark King in the Dark Corner. We can still recognize our friends, but we know that they're capable of doing the most horrid things because they have no control over their actions. You've come just in time, Deliah. It's getting worse, and we desperately need help. You are the blueprint. You are part of the prophecy: half-fairy, half-human. It's you who is needed. It's your destiny. Ostephen has volunteered to be your companion, and there will be many people and creatures that will help you along the way. Indeed you have the entire realm behind you."

"Why haven't your human friends helped?" Deliah asked.

Ostephen sighed and answered, "We do have human friends but not nearly enough to even begin to make a difference. For every human who believes in fairies, there are hundreds who don't. If only we could change this, there would be such harmony for us and for them. Until enough humans believe in our existence, they are unable to help us because our energy, our very existence feeds off of their belief. Unless enough of them choose to believe and help our energy build, they just don't hold enough power. We will ultimately vanish."

After finishing the plate of food, Deliah dusted herself off and was ready to set off on this unexpected and unexplainable journey. She was scared of the Dark Ones, and especially of reaching the Dark Corner, but she didn't hesitate to go because Papa's voice and her gut feelings confirmed that she was meant to be here for some reason. And Ostephen would be her companion, which made her happy. They had bonded quickly over their shared sorrow, and she knew they would be friends for life. So the little blue fairy and the little brave girl set out for the sunlight on a journey that would challenge two of the purest of souls.

Edwin

Chapter 4

A fairy is a tiny thing,
But there is nothing it can't bring.
Whatever you need ask for it,
In a sparkle of light you'll see us flit.

As they continued down the worn path, Deliah began to complain, "Is it getting hotter, or is it just me? I can barely move because the heat is so strong."

Ostephen's suspicions had begun to rise a mile back when the sky had suddenly turned a gloomy gray, but he didn't want to frighten her. Just then, he noticed a tiny, glowing red ember floating in the air. Suddenly, a rock knocked Deliah on the side of the head.

"Ow!" Deliah cried, rubbing her head. "That hurt!"

She turned around to see who was at fault when she heard Ostephen's shaky voice scream, "Run, Deliah! It's the Dark Ones!"

Without a moment's hesitation, Deliah followed Ostephen's light and dashed like mad for the water where, thanks to Cordelia's warning, she knew she could find safety with the merpeople. They heard the buzz of the Dark Ones behind them, taunting and terrifying. Their black cloud cast an eerie darkness over the entire land. With their red bodies and black clawed wings, they were frightening despite their small size. Their piercing, yellow eyes could cut right through you, paralyzing you with fear and dread. Truly they were exactly what one would imagine a good fairy gone bad might look like. Surrounded by a glow of flames, the only warning sign that they were near was the horrendous heat, ashes, and embers that filled the air. A painfully piercing screech filled Deliah's head as they got closer and closer. She tripped on the root of a tree, fell to her knees, and scrambled to find her footing again. Beads of sweat were dripping down her face and her back from the heat of the Dark Ones as they continued to close the gap.

"Hurry, Deliah! Just a few more feet!" Ostephen urged.

Deliah looked back at the army of Dark Ones and then plunged into the water, relieved to know that this was their only weakness. She stood waist deep, catching her breath, her heart slowly making its way back into her chest. Ostephen's glow being the only light, she looked at him and saw the terror etched across his kind, tiny face. She stretched out her hand, and he sat in her palm, trembling. The comforting sound of seashells began to rise and echo around them. As the merpeople began to emerge one by one and as the darkness faded away, Deliah released a huge sigh. She was safe; she was secure and completely protected. Gorgeous emerald green tails splashed against the surface of the water only to disappear and resurface moments later.

Ostephen's trembling subsided, but he knew he wouldn't feel better until he saw his best friend, Rosella. He informed Deliah that he needed to see his beloved friend, and he asked her to come along with him to the forest of pines a mile away. Deliah was in awe of the merpeople and encouraged him to go visit with Rosella while she lingered in the safety of the merpeople awhile longer.

"Don't worry. I'll find you as soon as I'm done," she promised. Ostephen knew no danger could find her there, so he left to see Rosella.

As Deliah waded to shore, she saw a mermaid perched high atop a rock, a landmark among the crystal clear waters. Deliah was drawn in by her serene singing voice and moved closer. This mermaid was unlike anything she'd ever seen. Her long, strawberry red-colored hair was set against ivory skin, and her neck was draped in pearls and shells of various shapes and colors. The mermaid's eyes were like looking glass, luring Deliah in only to mirror her own reflection. The mermaid's song calmed and captivated every sea creature within miles. It was so peaceful that Deliah couldn't help but drift off into a dream.

Lying on the shore, Deliah closed her eyes and relaxed.

Instantly clouds formed, and she imagined how it would feel to jump from one to another—big, soft, billowy cushions to always catch her fall. The mermaid's song drifted in and out of her dream like an orchestra of angels. The clouds formed different shapes and faces until Deliah thought she saw one that looked oddly familiar....

Papa? she wondered.

Her father's voice filled her head: I can only hope I've passed on to you the wisdom I've learned from my years of untruths. Learn from my life, but live your own, for you have the power to see the unknown.

Before she could say anything, the clouds parted, and her father vanished like a puff of smoke. Deliah slowly opened her eyes, wondering if that had been just a dream or if she had, in fact, heard Papa's voice. Her heart swelled, and her body tingled with a renewed strength; she could still feel his presence and decided that the encounter was no dream but was very real.

Deliah looked for the mermaid, but the rock was empty; she had left her perch. Splash! Deliah felt a few drops of water land on her face as the mermaid rose out of the water only a few feet before her and tossed Deliah a strand of sea green pearls.

In her serene voice, the mermaid softly whispered, "You are never alone, never lost—just on the journey. The bridge you must cross. Use the pearls; they are your own. They will enhance your power to see the unknown."

Then the mermaid gracefully glided back underwater, leaving Deliah to gather her thoughts and contemplate the afternoon's events. As she took a moment to look out at the still, green water, Deliah wrapped the beautiful strand of pearls around her wrist several times to make a bracelet. The pearls were so smooth and round. As she touched them, she saw a vision of a large bridge, but it didn't look very safe. She began to question the message, but *the bridge, the bridge* kept echoing in her ears.

I have to find Ostephen and see if he knows of a bridge, she resolved.

Before leaving, she silently thanked the merkingdom for their help before she set off toward the forest of pines to find Ostephen.

• • •

"Ostephen!" Rosella shouted joyously.

She was sitting on the branch of the oak tree she called home and was sewing something so large that it was draped over the entire branch. She quickly set her sewing aside, flew down, and gave him a big, warm hug; he relaxed in the safety and comfort she always provided. They had been close friends for years, and Rosella was the only one in whom Ostephen had found comfort after Kristoff was taken. She always seemed to know just what to say or do to make him feel better. Rosella had short brown pixie hair and dressed simply. She was considered plain by most.

"Why would I fuss over myself when I can spend that time helping others?" she would say.

When she did find time for herself, she was always cooking, reading, or sewing; she loved the creature comforts.

Ostephen asked her what on earth she was sewing, and she replied that it was a cloak for Deliah.

"Everyone is talking about her and the prophecy. I figured I would make her a nice gift for your journey. Besides it gets cold in the forest at night. I sewed in a couple pockets especially for you," she declared. She smiled, slightly blushing at Ostephen.

They flew up and sat together while she continued sewing, and he filled her in on their encounter with the Dark Ones. Rosella listened intently as she always did when he spoke, but upon hearing of his dangerous encounter, she flitted closer beside him and began checking his wings and his head, making sure he wasn't hurt. He enjoyed the attention, and the mood lightened as they began to recall old stories of Kristoff, Ostephen, and her playing. Finally, Rosella finished sewing the last of the gold lining on to the cloak.

Remembering Ostephen's directions, Deliah approached the oak tree and saw the two friends laughing while lounging on a branch.

"Hi!" Deliah shouted.

Ostephen took Rosella's hand and they flew down to greet her.

"Deliah! This is my beloved friend Rosella. Rosella, this is my new and dear friend Deliah," Ostephen said as he introduced them.

"Thank you for taking care of Ostephen. I do worry about

him," Rosella confessed.

Rosella looked at Ostephen with an undisguised longing, then her cheeks began to glow when she realized that Deliah had noticed, and she turned away. Deliah was taken with Rosella's simple beauty and knew they would become good friends.

"It's so very nice to meet you," Deliah replied, smiling.

"Rosella made you this."

Ostephen snapped his fingers, and Deliah suddenly felt her shoulders covered by a velveteen cloak. Startled, she ran her hands over the deep purple softness and the gold lining. She noticed it had several big pockets outside and secret pockets inside and thought it was positively grand. She pulled the soft velvet tighter around her tiny shoulders, appreciative of the instant warmth it provided.

"I like to sew, and I figured you could use the extra warmth. It'll keep you dry, too!" Rosella said humbly.

"It's wonderful! Thank you! You are so kind," Deliah said and smiled. "I've been wondering how it can be that a fairy—something so pure—can be turned to evil in the first place?" she asked them.

"It happens in a moment, dear Deliah," Ostephen said. "It is a choice in that moment of weakness when they give into temptation and release their power to the Dark Ones to get something they want more." He reached for a blackberry and took a big bite, chewing quickly so that he could finish answering her question. "By the time they even realize what happened, it's too late. This is why we must stop them before they turn too many and our kingdom is gone forever." Ostephen shuddered at the thought, and his blue eyes welled up with tears. "They took Kristoff, my brother. I must get him back! I must!"

"Don't worry. We'll find Kristoff. I promise."

When Deliah filled him in on the mermaid's message and her vision, Ostephen grabbed a twig and started to work out the directions to the nearest bridge in the dirt.

"So," he said, pointing the twig at a curvy line, "we must head east. Your vision was right. The bridge is old, but it shouldn't be too much of a problem. If we can't cross it, we'll just ask for Edwin."

"Edwin?" Deliah echoed curiously.

"You'll see...," he said over his shoulder as they waved goodbye to Rosella and set off.

• • •

Hours later, they came upon a very long, unkempt, and unsafe bridge.

"There are huge chunks of it missing!" Deliah cried in dismay. "What was the mermaid thinking? I can't cross this!"

She looked at the unwelcoming water below the bridge. The rocky ravine provided nothing to climb on or grab hold of. The only way to get across appeared to be the bridge. Deliah was so worried and tense that she almost cried.

"Ostephen, what are we going to do?"

All of a sudden, she heard chirping and turned around to see what had to be sixty or more swallows and meadowlark excitedly hopping from limb to limb in the trees. One of the small, beautiful birds fluttered directly in front of her, and to her astonishment, it began to speak.

"Beyond the horizon lies the truth. Come dawn you will seek it. Seek the truth, Deliah, and you will never be lost. Scan the horizon for signs. Fear is an illusion, dear child, remember this. Remember that *you* create your future. Choose trust; choose love. Edwin will help bear the weight of your travels. He will also serve as protection."

Deliah turned as she heard hooves coming from behind her.

"A unicorn!" she said under her breath in awe and disbelief. She had always loved unicorns, but, like fairies, she had believed they were only mythical.

Edwin was magnificent! His pure white coat reminded her of the first snowfall in winter. He had a shining rose crest on his forehead. He knelt down, and she ran her hand over his soft, silky coat. His horn gave off a soft glow like a rainbow-colored candle. Deliah was in a meditative state just looking at him. In fact, just being in Edwin's presence gave her great comfort and warmth. He neighed and tousled his gorgeous mane of white silk hair, and he told Deliah to hop on. She climbed on top of the unicorn. Feeling on top the world, Deliah leaned forward, hugging Edwin.

"Come on, Ostephen! Let's get your brother back!" she hollered as Ostephen settled into one of the pockets of her cloak.

Peering out, Ostephen nodded with determination. Under his breath, he mumbled, "I'm coming for you, Kristoff. I'm coming for you."

Edwin neighed excitedly, and with that, they took off, leaving just a faint glowing trail of color, the clacking of hooves, and the sixty-plus chirping birds behind them.

Deliah wasn't sure how they crossed the bridge, but Edwin had asked them to close their eyes and concentrate on reaching the other side. His horn became very bright; rainbow colors glowed, sparkled, and filled the air. As quickly as she had closed her eyes, they were safely across the bridge and on the other side. Ostephen took a moment to pray for her, Kristoff, and the entire journey ahead. Then he puffed out his little blue chest with a fake air of confidence and flew out of Deliah's pocket ready to meet the next obstacle.

Looking back across the expansive bridge, she couldn't help but feel a little nervous. They were stepping farther and farther away from home, but she knew there was no turning back; she wanted to help the fairies—she just *had* to. Edwin disappeared as quickly as he had come, but Ostephen assured Deliah that they hadn't seen the last of him.

They began walking through the forest when they heard an awful noise not far in the distance. Ostephen plugged his ears, and the two of them moved cautiously forward to see what was causing the horrible racket. As they got closer, they could hear machinery and could make out large shadowy figures with saws strewn about the forest. Still hidden in the trees, Deliah moved slightly closer and noticed several large, creepy creatures that looked somewhat like wolves but larger and meaner. Whatever they were, they were intimidating and looked very scary. Deliah quickly moved back and was startled to hear a low wail, a sad tormented cry. A horrible crashing thud made her jump, and peeking through a bunch of thick branches, she saw a perfect pine tree fall to the ground.

"Kahorgis, loyal followers of the Dark Ones," Ostephen whispered in hushed tones.

The Kahorgis were guffawing proudly as they cut down trees all over the forest. She felt so bad about the trees that she started to cry and was about to run out and make the Kahorgis stop, but Ostephen grabbed her.

"No, Deliah! We are no match for them! There's nothing we can do right now; it's too late for this forest."

His shoulders sank, and his ears shuddered at the sound of the crying trees. They watched in horror as several Kahorgis grabbed torches and set the felled pine on fire. They could hear the tree screaming in horror.

"Why? Why can't they see them? Why can't they hear them crying like I can?" Deliah asked, wiping her eyes.

Ostephen grabbed Deliah as they escaped the horrid scene. They knew they would never forget what they saw. She ran and ran until her legs went numb, and she fell to the ground with a thud. She was breathing hard, desperately trying to calm her nerves when she felt something envelop her body in a very secure and comforting hug. She instantly felt relief and calm. She didn't care who or what was hugging her; she was safe—something she hadn't felt for awhile. Rubbing her eyes, she looked up and saw that she was in the steady arms of an elm tree. She was so thankful to be safe that she turned around and smiled, and without a second thought, she wrapped her little arms as far as she could around its trunk and hugged it back. Two big eyes slowly blinked from beneath the bark. Among all the green leaves, she made out the well-camouflaged face of Green Man. It had been so long since she had received such a healing touch, it reminded her of Papa and how he used to pick her up and twirl her around before giving her a big hug every time he saw her.

Deliah sat wrapped in the arms of the elm, talking to Green Man for what seemed like hours, letting him absorb all her worries and fears. At times she felt guilty about unloading on one of nature's beautiful creations, but Green Man assured her that he was delighted to help and that it did not harm him in any way. Deliah shook her head, remembering the horrible sounds of crying trees.

"Why couldn't they hear them? Why couldn't they see their faces?" she asked.

"Dear Deliah, not all lights shine as bright as yours, I'm afraid."

"To think they could just cut them down like that, hurt them, and watch them die! Trees are just as alive as any other creature, are they not?" Deliah asked.

Green Man nodded his head in affirmation, sending a shower of leaves to the ground.

"Yes, they are very much alive. Every flower, every blade of grass is as alive as you and I. The thing you must focus on, Deliah, is that those trees did not die completely in vain. Although their life and beauty were cut short, they serve as a lesson that we can only hope others will one day learn. That we are all one; there is no one thing more worthy or alive than another. We are all family, all light, all love."

Feeling more relaxed, Deliah wiped away the last of her tears and hugged Green Man again. He smiled, knowing she was a true friend of the forest.

Raising her hand to her heart, she thanked Green Man for everything.

As he slowly closed his bark-covered eyes, he whispered, "The Silver Star. You must find the Silver Star."

Frog Prince

Chapter 5

When you're in touch with nature,
All shall become clear.
We promise you'll find nothing but love and truth here.
Come back and visit; we'll share with you.
Until then, we'll frolic as fairies are wont to do.

Deliah and Ostephen were meandering their way through the forest when they saw a flowery fairy flying in their direction.

"Yoo-hoo! Yoo-hoo!" she was calling and waving excitedly in their direction.

"Mayweather, hello!" they greeted her warmly.

"Ah, I thought I saw you two. I was just helping a friend nearby with some of her roses. Poor things got sprayed by human pesticide and nearly died! She's been trying to give the human signs for months, but they don't seem to be getting it. Why she even hid their can of the awful chemicals, and they just bought a new one! Imagine that!" She shook her head in total disbelief. "Well, word is your heading for the Silver Star. You'll get there faster if you pass through Froglany. If it's all right with you, I thought you might let this old fairy tag along for some fun?"

"We'd love to have you join us," they both said in unison. As they marched onward, Deliah wasn't scared anymore; she was just plain determined. She began walking heavily and slamming her feet into the ground as though it were a Kahorgi, her worst enemy. She took another forceful step when she heard a weeping sound. "Did you hear that?" she asked.

"Oh, yeah. That's just Weepin' Willy," they replied nonchalantly. "You get used to him after awhile."

They pointed toward a Caragana willow tree, and Deliah realized she was stomping on one of his roots.

"Oh, dear! I'm terribly sorry," Deliah blurted apologetically.

"Oh, it's not you. Don't wo...worry," he said in between sobs. Deliah looked to the fairies, confused, but they just shrugged.

"They call him Weepin' Willy because all he ever does is weep," Ostephen explained.

The weeping Caragana reached out a branch to greet Deliah and with eyes full of sympathy, she looked into Weepin' Willy's wet, tired eyes.

"Is there anything I can do?" she asked earnestly.

"No," he said in a wobbly voice, "I just c...can't stop cr... crying...."

"Watch out, me dear," Mayweather pointed down, warning Deliah of stepping in a nearby puddle of Willy's tears. Deliah stepped back, slightly unsure of what to do. She just couldn't leave him; he was so sad!

"Go on n...now," Weepin' Willy said. "Don't you wo... worry about me. I'll be fine. We all appreciate what y...you're doing for the k...kingdom."

Deliah smiled sincerely, and she could tell Willy wanted to tell her something, but he stopped himself.

"Move along, sweet ch...ch...child. Bless ya," he said.

Deliah found it odd that such a vibrant, well-grown tree was so terribly sad.

"Bye, Weepin' Willy," Deliah said regretfully as she took off to catch up with the fairies. "I'll come back and visit when all this is over!" she called out before silently saying a little prayer for Willy.

"People try and guess why he cries," Ostephen said. "Some think he cries for the trees they've lost, some think it is for his parents who were cut down, and others think he simply likes the attention."

"Didn't seem like that to me," Deliah said defensively. "I'm pretty sure he'd feel grand if he could stop weeping."

She couldn't explain it, but something about him had

touched her heart. He wasn't needy or grieving; he seemed under some kind of spell, and she was going to help him out of it. But now was not the time. She had to get to the Silver Star, and the first stop would be Froglany to talk to the frog prince. Mayweather had assured them that Froglany would provide the quickest access to the Silver Star and that it was much too fun not to visit.

A few miles later, Ostephen whispered with a little blush in his voice, "Oh, look! We've reached Lovers' Lilies!"

Deliah looked out at the moonlit water full of heart-shaped lily pads floating atop with couples side by side. Some were cuddling; some were kissing; and others had their legs outstretched and their arms behind their heads, staring at the stars.

Deliah giggled and said, "Oh, my! I had no idea frogs were so romantic."

Mayweather sighed jealously and said, "Oh, they are, dear. Lovers' Lilies is one of the most romantic spots in Faye." Deliah heard a frog singing tenor and pushing his lily pad along as though it were a gondola floating down a canal in Venice. "Let's just sit and rest for a minute, shall we?" Mayweather asked already seated. "It's such a gorgeous view! We shan't let it go to waste," she said, trying to mask her longing.

They sat in the long grass surrounded by bulrushes, all huddled close together as if they were on their own giant lily pad on the shore, hoping to one day float down Lovers' Lilies as happy as the rest of the couples. After a few moments and sighs from Mayweather, they dusted themselves off and started toward the encroaching music.

"The band's startin'!" Ostephen said gleefully. "Best mariachi band in the land! If there's one thing frogs know how to do, it's throw a party!" Deliah heard Mexican music overtaking the frog's tenor voice as lights and laughter filled the cool night air.

"Ay yay yay!" a frog shouted from the stage, tapping his webbed foot to the beat.

"It's magnificent!" Deliah gushed as she twirled around, arms out, taking in the festivities and colors.

The mariachi band was the cutest thing she'd ever seen, and it was obvious that they were the rock stars of Froglany. Lady frogs crowded the stage with roses in hand, blowing kisses and winking at the band. There was an endless number of dragonflies lighting up the night sky with their beautiful red, blue, orange, purple, and yellow hues.

Just as she was about to take a seat on a nearby log, Deliah heard a deep throaty voice ask, "May I?"

Someone politely took her by the hand, and she flinched at the unexpected wet and slimy feel. She looked down to see the green, webbed hand of a frog; she looked up to see a brilliant, golden crown.

"The frog prince!" she exclaimed.

"Yes, ma'am," he said as he bowed and kissed her on the hand. "You've arrived just in time for the festivities, I see."

Before Deliah had a chance to respond, he took her other hand and spun her into his arms, whisking her off into the middle of the dance floor.

Ostephen looked for Mayweather who seemed to have disappeared altogether. He found her sulking on a nearby bench as she watched Deliah dance with the frog prince.

"Don't tell me you're jealous of Deliah dancing with a frog," he said accusingly.

"Oh, hush up!" she mumbled as she waved her hand, brushing him off. "Not at all," she continued while dabbing at her eye with a broad leaf.

Ostephen gave an exaggerated bow before her and with teasing eyes and mocking tones said, "Mayweather, you look exceptional this evening. Might you do me the honor?"

"Oh, Ostephen, you bet your little blue butt I will!"

Mayweather dropped her leaf on the log. And with that, they were off to join Deliah and the frog prince.

"Ay yay yay!" the singer shouted again. Everyone was shaking and dancing, hands in the air, swaying from side to side. After all, if there's one thing the frogs are known for, it's their parties.

"So are you like the frog prince from fairy tales?" Deliah asks tentatively.

"Are you wondering if I'll turn into a human prince if you kiss me?"

"Well, no, just if you were ever human?"

"No, I'm forever a frog prince—born of royal frog parents in Froglany, I'm afraid. However, if you'd like to kiss me, it couldn't

36

hurt to try," he said, puckering up.

The song ended much to Deliah's relief, and she nervously thanked him for the dance and eagerly turned her attention to the band, clapping continually. The frog prince, who was not shy and who enjoyed a challenge, shrugged and laughed to himself, knowing that he had clearly made her uncomfortable.

"He's one smooth frog, that one," Mayweather said, directing Ostephen's eyes to the prince.

"Yeah, well, Deliah would never fall for a frog. That much I know," Ostephen scoffed.

The frog prince left to get Deliah a drink and then headed back toward her with a coconut cup garnished with a vibrant red flower. Before he could reach her, Ostephen buzzed in front of him, sat on the side of the cup, and leaned in to take a large slurp. Disgusted, the frog prince tossed the drink aside.

Ostephen flew in front of his face and asked scoffingly, "So, prince...charming, is it?"

The prince smiled, well aware of his own charm. He replied, "No, no, little guy. Just prince." Then he waved Ostephen away. The frog prince dusted off his formal jacket and straightened his collar as he smoothly sent glances to all the ladies. When Ostephen saw Mayweather waving back to the prince like a smitten kitten, he decided it may be time to move on from Froglany.

"So, prince, are you going to help us? Or should we just move along?"

"Help?" the prince asked confused.

"Yes, I'm sure you're aware of the blueprint. Deliah is the one guided here to help. We need to reach the Silver Star."

The frog prince now stood even taller as though he were king of a great land about to address his public. He cleared his throat dramatically, and a frog barely half the prince's size signaled for the band to stop. A hush fell over the crowd.

"My dear and loyal friends and visitors of Froglany, I would like to introduce to you Deliah, the savior." All the frogs clapped and cheered for her. Looking at Deliah, he continued, "Rest assured, all of Froglany will be at your side if ever you need us."

Deliah made her way through the crowd of frogs toward the frog prince, curtsied politely before him, and thanked him for his help. Looking at Ostephen, who had followed her, she could

37

tell it was time to go.

"Thank you so much for your hospitality and fun. I won't forget it, but I'm afraid we have run out of time and must continue our journey."

The frog prince put an arm around Deliah's shoulder and revealed Froglany's hidden canals to Deliah in hushed tones. "You will reach the Silver Star much faster and safer this way. I wish you to use them."

"Thank you so much," Deliah replied. "I'd be honored."

"Now I should warn you, Deliah, that the Silver Star is more important than you realize. It is a portal and will help further your journey. You will come to a point when you see nothing but dark, starlit sky. You must trust your intuition and find the destined Silver Star. When you've found it, you must jump immediately. Don't hesitate, or you could lose your opportunity. Just jump toward the star, Deliah, and you will arrive at your destination."

Starting to feel nervous again but thankful for the information, Deliah shook the hand of the frog prince. He immediately grabbed her and enveloped her in a hug. After what felt like ages, he unwrapped his wet and slimy arms from the hug, bowed graciously, and assigned one of his servants to lead her to the hidden canal.

The swamp was dark and squishy and would be easy to get lost in, but they marched onward. The dark canal seemed to go on forever without many distinctions.

Ostephen started to complain that his wings were getting tired when the prince's servant announced, "This is as far as I go. Go forward three more miles, stop, turn five times, and then take four steps backward and seven steps forward. Good luck." He bowed, placing a tiny webbed foot before the other.

Deliah looked from Mayweather to Ostephen, hoping someone caught all that. She saw Mayweather's lips moving: "three...five...four...seven..." Deliah stifled a giggle.

"Does everything have to be a riddle, Ostephen?" Deliah asked.

"It's not about riddles; it's about games, mystery, and— yes—some mischief, too."

Mayweather added, "You'll soon see that often what seems like a riddle here is actually more straightforward and logical than anything in the human realm."

As they approached the third-mile mark, they came into a clearing, and Deliah began to walk slower, not on purpose but because she was entranced by the stars. There was nothing but dark sky and shining silver stars for miles. After Papa passed away, Deliah used to lie in the grass out back and stare up at the stars. For some reason, it made her feel better. They had the same effect on her now, and she suddenly surrendered any worries she had about finding the destined Silver Star. She felt connected to the stars, and she knew Papa would help her.

Papa, she said to herself, I'm going to need your help. I'm going to need you. I don't want to let my friends down...or you.

At the end of the three-mile walk, they all stopped, looked at one another, and began to turn five times, Mayweather still mouthing the numbers to herself. They stopped turning and slowly took four steps back. One cautious foot in front of another, they took seven carefully planted steps forward. There they were: the backs of two little fairies and one little girl against a dark, starlit sky and the most unlikely of trios ready to take on the universe. Ostephen and Mayweather bowed their heads in silent prayer, knowing that events were out of their hands. It was up to Deliah to find the Silver Star. Her gift of intuition was much stronger, and it was her destiny.

A hazy smoke began to cloud some of the stars, and the smell of burning wood filled the air. Deliah thought she saw a star sparkle but quickly realized it was an ember.

"The Dark Ones!" they all screamed.

The heat once again began to creep up on them from all directions. Sweat started pouring down their foreheads. Mayweather dabbed a crocheted hankie at her forehead despite the impending doom. The fairies looked at Deliah terrified.

"They're getting close, Deliah! We need the star!" Ostephen yelled.

Deliah looked back at the army of Dark Ones buzzing behind followed by their loyal Kahorgis. The three of them were way outnumbered.

She panicked, then remembered Papa's voice: *You have the power to see the unknown.*

She stared at the stars, rubbing the mermaid's bracelet,

searching for the Silver one, but all she could hear was Papa's voice whispering in her ear.

The Dark Ones were well within reach, and Ostephen and Mayweather's wings began wilting from the intense heat. They were beginning to fade, almost too weak even to fly. A Dark One buzzed in front of Deliah, and as she ducked, it circled Mayweather. The tail end of the flame singed her wing, and she began to fall to the ground. Ostephen quickly buzzed under her and caught her, but he couldn't carry her for long.

"Deliah!" he yelled in alarm.

Just as a Kahorgi stomped and was about to lash out at Deliah's left arm, she looked up and saw an unusual sparkle. The Silver Star! Quickly taking hold of Ostephen and Mayweather with her right hand, she leapt forward, their arms and legs spread wide like three starfish flying through the night sky. The Kahorgi gave an enraged snarl; he had missed her by mere inches.

Laflin

Chapter 6

The fairies dance, play, and sing,
For this is how they create the joy they bring.

The three unsung heroes fell into a tunnel of blinding silver light before landing hard on their bottoms. Deliah opened her eyes and looked around to take in an etched wooden signpost.

"Luminous Lane," she uttered as she turned round to see the splendor of the land. "What a cozy, candlelit place indeed!"

The only light came from candles, but they were not your ordinary candles. There were thousands of white-winged candles flying and hovering in the air all around them.

"They're like little angel candles," Deliah said aloud. Just then, she heard a grunt and turned to see Mayweather's struggle to get up despite her burnt wing. "Oh my goodness!" she cried, "Are you all right?"

Always a trooper, Mayweather tried to shrug it off, but with her singed wing, she was incapable of flying, and a grimace of pain managed to escape her clenched lips. Ostephen tried to help her up but realized she needed more help than he could give.

"Okay. I know a healer here who can help her. She lives at 123 Luminous Lane. Let's go," he said hurriedly. He helped Mayweather onto Deliah's outstretched palm, and they quickly moved down the lane, searching the well-marked cottages, looking for the one marked *123*.

"Here we are," Ostephen shouted happily. "Mrs. McCullum, the healer, lives here. Her husband is Laflin, the leprechaun."

42

Hearing a chipper, hearty laugh inside, Deliah knocked on the door with her free hand, but no one answered. She knocked louder, and suddenly the door swung wide open. As soon as Mrs. McCullum saw Ostephen standing there, she shrieked happily. Then with barely a glance, she spotted Mayweather's wing.

"Hurry in, my dears," she commanded sweetly, ushering them inside. "Let's mend this poor thing, shall we? Ostephen, it's so wonderful to see you. It's been so long. I still feel badly...," her voice trailed off in sadness and disappointment.

Ostephen whispered to Deliah, "I thought she might be able to help me help Kristoff, but...." His eyes began to tear up, so he looked sadly at the floor, and Deliah squeezed his little blue hand.

"And you must be Deliah. I knew our paths would be crossin'. The leaves told me as much."

Mrs. McCullum gave Deliah a hearty hug and turned back to her injured patient. Mayweather, who had started yawning minutes ago as Mrs. McCullum pressed a damp cloth to her forehead, had now fallen fast asleep. While she slept, Mrs. McCullum tenderly patted her burnt wing with loving care and a lotion that smelled of sandalwood. The healer also wrapped Mayweather in a warm tea towel, which she calculated was tiny enough to serve as a blanket. She then gathered Deliah and Ostephen into the kitchen where she began brewing some tea.

Another bout of uproarious laughter bellowed through the house, startling the lot of them.

"Laflin!" Mrs. McCullum shouted. "Keep it down! We have guests, and you're about to wake one from a much-needed slumber. Now, my dears, how are you two?"

Mrs. McCullum was a robust woman, though she was quite short as Laflin was. Indeed, she, too, resembled a leprechaun. She had a warm, freckled face; red hair; and sincere, light blue eyes. They were about to fill her in on their latest adventure when Laflin entered the kitchen.

"Take your hat off," Mrs. McCullum said. "'Tis rude otherwise."

Laflin put his right hand to his belly over the top of his black belt and green coat and laughed. Then he received a warning glance from the missus and promptly removed his green top hat. They'd been together for years, and Laflin knew just how far he could push her, as she did him. This was what made their relationship work; they kept each other on their toes.

After Ostephen introduced Deliah to Laflin, they all settled in for a nice pot of tea, complete with tea leaves, which Mrs. McCullum informed them she would be reading at the end of each cup.

"'Tis an ancient art, tea leaf reading," Ostephen whispered to Deliah.

Deliah took her last sip with both hands wrapped around the cup before sliding the cup across the table to Mrs. McCullum, who turned the cup around and over and then looked intently into Deliah's face. Suddenly, Mrs. McCullum looked stricken.

"Well, goodness!" she took a deep breath, then fell silent. "In all my years...."

"Nice work, kid. You managed to make her speechless. I've been trying to accomplish that for years!" Laflin snorted.

Just then, the cup rose out of Mrs. McCullum's hands and hovered in the air amid the candles. It began to shake and rattle before it shattered and turned into confetti. The colorful confetti slowly fell to the center of the table, forming a few odd wavy lines that only Mrs. McCullum seemed to understand.

She studied them for a moment then said, "Color. Color and celebration, child. There's going to be some kind of a celebration in Greenland!"

After spending the night in Mrs. McCullum's warm and welcoming home, they awoke refreshed and ready to continue on their journey. Because Mayweather was still weak and needed to heal, Mrs. McCullum insisted that she stay behind. After a plentiful breakfast and more laughs, Laflin sneakily tucked a few gold coins into Deliah's hand when the missus wasn't looking.

"It will serve ya down the road," he said with a wink.

With that, Deliah and Ostephen wished Mayweather well and headed down Luminous Lane toward Greenland.

"It's hard to tell what time it is with only candlelight to follow," Deliah said to Ostephen.

In unison, they echoed, "It's beautiful!"

The candles seemed to sense their presence and followed them down Luminous Lane, happy to provide extra light. As they approached the end of the lane and the beginning of the Irish

Bush People

countryside, they turned around to say goodbye. The candle flames all flickered at once as if to reply and wish them well. Looking out at the never-ending trees and clear blue sky, they began to hum and whistle their way onward to Greenland, praying that encounters with Kahorgis would be far off or nonexistent.

• • •

About half a mile up, Ostephen stopped abruptly, gripping Deliah's right arm tightly. She could tell something was wrong and followed his gaze to a little yellow fairy surrounded by two Dark Ones. The fairy was stealing an abundance of berries from a nearby bush, kicking pinecones, and throwing rocks at the trees. He was being very unkind toward the forest. Ostephen's blue lips started to quiver as he looked Deliah in the eye.

"No," Deliah said, "it can't be...."

"Kristoff!" Ostephen whispered ashamed.

Kristoff flew across the path, a small trail of flames behind him. He laughed as he set fire to a pile of leaves. Deliah grabbed Ostephen and hid behind a bush so that they would not be spotted. She patted Ostephen's leg, knowing how hard it must be to see his brother be so unkind. She silently wished she could do something to stop them, but she and Ostephen were outnumbered, so all they could do was hide. As the three vandals made their way through the forest, they continued to burn various bushes, leaving a horrid burnt smell behind them.

Still crouched behind the bush, she saw the two Dark Ones get knocked by a few large pinecones and put her hand to her mouth to stifle a gasp. The pinecones hit the ground and caught fire. The Dark Ones buzzed even louder, trying to intimidate the unseen enemy, but a cascade of pinecones continued to rain down upon them. With a flash of flame, Kristoff and the Dark Ones retreated, knowing they were momentarily outnumbered.

Deliah looked up, wondering where the pinecones had come from.

"Oh my!" she exclaimed as she saw what appeared to be small green creatures about a foot and a half in height with flat noses, squishy faces, and live grass for hair.

Their arms and legs were stout and stumpy but adorably round. They moved quite methodically, their grassy hair flowing with the breeze. She noticed that they made a squishy sound when they moved and that they jumped from tree to tree. She followed the squishy sound and saw one land on the path in front of her followed by a few others.

"We're bush people, friends of the forest," he announced, "and friends of yours."

Ostephen came out from behind the bush, shoulders hung sadly, looking to the earth.

"We're sorry, Ostephen," the bush people said. "We're watching Kristoff for you; we know it's not really him. He knows not what he does. He's always been a dear friend of the forest. You both have."

"Thanks," Ostephen mumbled. He was grateful that they had gone out of their way to miss Kristoff in their defense of the forest.

"We're everywhere," they said, "and we'll always keep an eye out for ya. The sun is beginning to set. Let us provide you with a lantern or a compass of sorts."

Suddenly, a little dragonfly buzzed over. It was encased in a rectangle of twigs, which formed a triangle roof. He hovered happily in the middle above a single lily. The bush people explained that all Deliah needed to do was request light, and it would be provided. The dragonfly seemed to smile back at her, happy to help. She looked at the bush people and wondered how it worked as a compass.

"See the lily? Well, the closer you get to your destination, the more the flower blooms; the farther you get, the closer to doom."

"Wow! That's extraordinary!" Deliah exclaimed. "Thanks!"

The bush people jumped back up into the trees and waved goodbye with their squat, stubby arms. Deliah was very grateful for their loyalty and their protection on the journey. She waved back, picked up Ostephen, and set him on her shoulder. Then she picked up the dragonfly lantern and eagerly continued down the path.

Deliah looked down at the lily and saw it slowly blooming beneath the dragonfly's golden light. Ostephen hadn't spoken much at all; his sadness over seeing Kristoff with the Dark Ones was really taking its toll. He hadn't moved from Deliah's shoulder. He just remained glum with his head hung low. Deliah had tried to make the odd joke or point out something funny to distract him, but he had yet to crack a smile. Struggling to find her way with her silent companion, she had decided to keep steady on the same path. She began to grow sleepy from all the walking and yawned. The sun had set, and she was grateful for the lantern.

Ostephen had fallen asleep, and Deliah had considered stopping and waiting for him to wake up, but she wanted to reach Greenland as soon as possible if for no other reason than to get Ostephen back to his usual self. He'd mentioned Greenland to her before. The gnomes lived there, including his good friend Herbie. His face had lit up every time he mentioned it.

An hour or so had passed, and Deliah paused to catch her breath. Leaning on a tree trunk, she searched her surroundings for some kind of sign to help her on her way. The lily had stopped blooming, and Deliah knew she should wake Ostephen, but her stubborn, independent side wanted to prove she could find her way alone. She spotted a wooden sign post that read *Greenland— this way* with an arrow. It seemed odd to her that she hadn't noticed a sign like that before, but she reasoned it was probably a fairy or forest friend helping her out. She had been receiving guidance and help from several forest friends, so she reasoned that the sign must be okay and marched onward following the sign.

A mile or so later, the dragonfly continued to try to get Deliah's attention, hovering lower above the lily which was now closing, but Deliah was lost in her own world, practically sleepwalking. She felt sticky beads of sweat dripping down her forehead and wiped them away with her sleeve. She thought to herself that she'd made good progress, having followed three more signs with arrows. Deliah now felt so weak and tired from the increasing heat that she gave in to a final yawn and settled under a sugar tree that sparkled with white twinkling lights made even more beautiful by the moonlight. Like cherry and orange trees, sugar trees had been around forever in Faye. If you found a sugar tree, you could pick your favorite fresh sweet: cupcakes, cookies, tarts, and candies galore.

As Deliah got even sleepier, she thought, I'll have to pick one of those cupcakes and put a chocolate in my pock—….

Thrilled that their signs had worked and had led Deliah down the wrong path, the group of Dark Ones crept closer in the night. Surrounded by their glowing flames, they smiled sinfully as they pictured how proud the Dark King would be when they captured Deliah and brought her back to the castle. The six of them continued to creep toward her and were just about to cast the capture spell on her when they were pushed back several yards by a mighty rush of water and fell to the ground. They angrily got up and armed themselves for a fight but were again stunned senseless by another wave of water and saw Edwin the unicorn's horn beaming through the forest at them. He stood protectively in front of Deliah, rubbing his hooves in the dirt as though he were about to charge at them. Unicorns were a symbol of power and purity, and even a Dark One would not dare attempt an attack on a unicorn. Many Dark Ones had tried and failed. Gasping in the water for air and struggling to fly out with their wet, withered wings, they buzzed bitterly. Edwin stood his ground with a grace even a swan would admire. Sensing his victory, Edwin at last stopped the flow of water and watched as the six drenched Dark Ones, sore and sullen, stumbled away.

Having woke up to the sound of waves of water and miserable shrieks, Ostephen and Deliah sat huddled behind Edwin and wondered what on earth had just happened.

Edwin bowed his long neck and mane slightly in acknowledgement before saying, "I urge you to be more careful, dear child. You needn't try to figure things out on your own. If you are lost or unsure, know that it takes more courage to ask for help than it does to deny it."

Feeling quite embarrassed at her own stubbornness, Deliah nodded quietly and thanked him. Ostephen opened the door of the lantern and looked at the now closed, wilted lily. The dragonfly who still hovered above it gave him a look of "Hey, I tried" before buzzing out of the lantern and flying away.

Edwin offered to help Deliah and Ostephen get to Greenland, which would make up for any lost time. They eagerly accepted and climbed on his back. They were staring at the sun setting over the rolling green hills and brilliant bright flowers of Greenland in what seemed like mere seconds. The land was filled with tulips and colorful flowers in bloom. Woodpeckers and birds of all kinds nested in the trees, and the sky was bluer than anything Deliah had ever seen. It seemed Greenland was graced with a little extra cast of color.

Chapter 7

To dewdrops and rainbows and sparkles anew,
To fairies, elves, and unicorns, too,
To all the great creatures that roam through Faye,
To the many wonders that surround us each day.

There was a buffet of food, drink, music, and dancing as various fairies, leprechauns, elves, foxes, and elemental friends waved them over and invited them to join the fun. They knew of Deliah and her journey, and they were happy to provide some food and respite. Deliah asked the fairies and friends what the celebration was about, and they all fell over laughing and wondered why humans always needed a cause for a celebration.

"You guys are certainly social," Deliah said to Ostephen, feeling embarrassed.

"Oh, indeed," Ostephen said with a nod.

A song started up, and he placed his right hand to his heart and began reciting the national anthem of Faye.

"Run through the grass with reckless abandon. Let down your hair in true fairy fashion. We live for the joy, the games, and the laughter, for, you see, these are your keys to happily ever after," he crooned, smiling proudly.

Suddenly, Ostephen spotted Rosella and flew over to give her a big hug. She was just as happy to see him and set down the cap she had been knitting him. She urged him to sit down and rest, while she gathered food and drink for him.

"Deliah!" Ostephen called, waving Deliah over.

Deliah was happy to see Rosella again. And after Ostephen got pulled away and into the crowd by a gnome, the two ladies easily fell into conversation. Deliah watched Rosella's eyes follow Ostephen into the crowd.

"He's lucky to have such a good friend," Deliah said.

With a knowing smile, Rosella looked to Deliah and said, "He loves me. He just doesn't know it yet." Deliah nodded, and the two giggled.

The group of elementals began to gather around Deliah, and they informed her that there was actually another reason for their meeting up with her.

"We are here to teach you the skill of foresight," they explained. "We will help you practice your breathing and concentration. You will need it when you reach the Dark Corner."

With that, they all settled in. As a group, they taught Deliah how to ignore distractions and listen to her own voice. They showed her how to slow her breathing and focus when she was faced with fear and how to find calm in any moment. It was frustrating for Deliah at first; she found it hard to quiet her mind and concentrate, but they all assured her that she was a natural and that the more she practiced, the easier it would become. The more fear the Dark Ones can sense, the stronger they feel. This is why it is best to breathe and concentrate on what you want to happen, not what you fear will happen. Deliah petted the fox beside her and thanked the group for their help. She felt good knowing she had a skill to rely on when she reached the Dark Corner.

Hours later, they were still mingling and having fun with their allies and friends. One fairy, dressed as a ballerina, danced over to Deliah. While winking and twirling, the fairy handed her a piece of chocolate cake.

"I'm Ballencia. Dance and sing; be merry for our sake. Enjoy life, for it is a piece of cake!"

She laughed and spun as Deliah accepted the cake. Ballencia was so graceful that she never walked; she always danced, and if she didn't dance, she glided. Her little pink tutu and ballet slippers were sparkly and drew attention, but there was nothing about Ballencia that was insincere or needy. She was just full of life—a reminder to the other fairies of the beauty and fun in every step of every moment.

I think I may take up ballet when I get home, Deliah thought, suddenly inspired. *If I ever get home…*, she heard a voice in her head threaten. She suddenly envisioned Grandma still sleeping soundly by the fire. *I'll be back, Grandma*, she vowed silently. *I won't leave you.*

Deliah suddenly froze as she held a vision of the Dark Ones buzzing toward her grandmother's house. Within a few feet of the door, she saw them slam against an invisible wall and angrily retreat. She breathed a sigh of relief, seeing that Tatum was inside laughing and reading a book next to Grandma. Coming out of her vision, Deliah took a big bite of the yummy cake and looked around at all the frolicking fairies.

I wonder where Ostephen has gone? she mused.

Ostephen slumped down on a smooth, flat bedrock. Resting his chin in his hands, he thought glumly, *Here we go again*. Every time he would gain confidence and prepare to make his move, something or someone would swoop in and nullify all his efforts.

Forget it, he said to himself, *This is what it is and what it will always be*. He sipped the last of his berry juice, his only comfort at the moment. Looking around at all the other couples dancing, singing, and drinking merrily, his heart heaved with an undeserved heaviness, a loneliness that had been eating away at him for far too long. As always, his gaze slowly drifted back to Ballencia. Her long blonde hair cascaded over her shoulders like silk. Her laugh haunted him as did the flirtatious glimmer in her icy blue eyes. She caught him staring and waved him over, never one to shy away from a moment's admiration. Suddenly released from his sullen state, Ostephen set his mug down in the grass and was about to hop to when *he* swooped in, took her by the hand, and twirled her around the dance floor.

Slumping back down onto his rock, Ostephen rolled his big blue eyes, sighed wearily, and muttered an infuriated, "Nad!"

He hated to admit it, but he was jealous of Nad. Nad had no problems getting attention from the lady fairies; they all swooned. His orange glow was hard to compete with, and he was always working out—or showing off, as Ostephen chose to see it—but there was no denying that Nad was definitely one fit fairy. Ostephen once thought of joining Nad for a workout or asking him for some advice, but he couldn't bring himself to do it. Ostephen wished he had it in him to get up and steal Ballencia away from Nad. Ostephen could take Nad on if it came to that— at least Ostephen hoped he could. It didn't matter. Ostephen shrugged because he knew he never would.

He looked up as a group of fairies challenged Nad to break his jumping record. A bunch of fairies were all piled atop one another's shoulders, creating a line that reached six feet high. They were all cheering loudly, "Nad, Nad, Nad, Nad…!"

Oh, come on! Ostephen thought.

"He'll never make it!" someone at the bottom of the pile shouted.

"Remember, no wings!" Ballencia yelled.

Nad was ready; knees bent, crouched, and focused.

He'll make it, Ostephen said to himself. *He always does.*

Sure enough, with no wings, Nad managed to jump up and over, making it look effortless. The fairies all fell over one another, laughing and cheering hysterically. This was one of their favorite games at every fairy party.

Ostephen sighed. "Yeah, great job!" he muttered sarcastically. "Real impressive orange glow."

Then he froze as he spotted a swoosh of long blonde hair and saw his beautiful fairy lean in and kiss Nad adoringly on the cheek. Ostephen's light dimmed to almost nothing. He was loved and adored by the rest of the realm, commonly referred to as "the good one." No one had ever met a gentler, generous soul. He was fairly happy, had a great family and good friends, but none of that mattered because the love he so yearned for still escaped him. Hiding his tenderhearted face, he dragged himself through the forest, ignorant of its simple pleasures: the sweet smell of the pine trees and the crunching of their needles beneath his pointy-toed feet. Ostephen needed to rest; a new day would soon dawn.

It was sunrise when Deliah awoke to find Ostephen missing. As she was looking about in a panic, a little bluebird chirped her a good morning and filled her in on his whereabouts.

"I saw him this morning as I was gathering worms for the youngins. He's okay. He came back late, and he's sleeping right by that cherry tree over there."

Deliah followed the bluebird and found Ostephen sleeping slumped against the cherry tree, murmuring of Ballencia and then Kristoff. She assumed that he must have been dreaming and felt it best to leave him for awhile longer and allow him some extra slumber. She decided to go for a walk and pick some fruit from a nearby cove to bring along for the next part of their journey. As she stretched on her tiptoes trying to knock down a pear from an orchard, she noticed a thin red puff of smoke float by her. She suddenly fell to the ground limp and unconscious.

Sidney, the squirrel who had been gathering nuts nearby, witnessed the whole event and scurried off to get help.

"Poison! Poison! The little girl's been poisoned!" his tiny voice shrieked as he ran through the forest. Ostephen opened his eyes to see what all the racket was as Sidney skidded to a halt in front of him. "She…sh…sh…poi….She was…."

"Spit it out," Ostephen said. Sometimes he got annoyed with the squirrels; they were very anxious and scattered.

"Deliah! She got…Dark One…poison!"

Ostephen flew up immediately and followed Sidney, flying as fast as his little wings would allow. He arrived at the base of the pear tree and saw Deliah's lifeless body.

"Help!" he shouted. "Help!"

He buzzed from one direction to the other, frantically searching for someone or something. Just then, he saw a group of gnomes making their way over the hill on their way back from the pond and recognized his friend Herbie.

"Help! Herbie! The Dark Ones! They poisoned her!" he shrieked.

The gnomes heard his cry and trudged faster toward him. The gnomes lifted Deliah up above their heads.

"If there's any hope for her at all, it's in the crystal cave. Hurry!" They trekked quickly to the west for about a quarter of a mile. Their short arms were getting tired, but they were hard workers and never once complained. The crystal cave had been around for centuries; it was the home of many miraculous healings.

"Hurry!" Ostephen shouted worriedly. "She hasn't got much time!"

The gnomes finally approached the healing cave and rushed Deliah in. Hands held high above little gnome heads, they continue to carry her in as though they were a well-formed assembly line.

The cave looked like the aurora borealis, and the colors kept changing: red to orange to yellow to green to blue to purple and back to red. Merely being inside the crystal cave caused Ostephen's fears to subside slightly. The cave's healing powers were written about centuries ago; it was legendary. It just had to help her. Slowly fluttering along, his eyes blinking with trepidation, Ostephen knew all would be well. They'd come this far. He felt certain that the universe would not disappoint them.

A rich green hue took over the cave, and the gnomes stopped and gently placed her on the crystal ground. The green lights encircled her entire body, swirling in all directions until her body lifted from the floor, and the green light entered her mouth, her eyes, and her ears. Her body was wrapped in a cocoon of emerald green crystal. Herbie, the head gnome, let a tiny squeal of awe slip from his lips. Ostephen sat on Herbie's shoulder, his little blue hand held to his heart in hope.

Suddenly, Deliah disappeared as a thick mist of green clouded everything and everyone. The mist began to fade, and the gnomes shuffled forward anxious for some sign of life. The mist continued to settle, but there was no sign of Deliah. Ostephen's hand fell to his lap, and Herbie patted it lovingly with compassion. The cave had returned to its normal kaleidoscope of colors. The gnomes looked from one to another with saddened faces, not sure what to say or do.

Herbie finally said, "I'm sorry, Ostephen."

"Ostephen!" they heard Deliah's voice shout enthusiastically. They looked toward the opposite end of the cave. Beyond a blinding white light, they made out a tiny figure running toward them.

"Deliah!" they shouted in disbelief. "It worked! It truly worked!"

Herbie and Ostephen ran to embrace Deliah, and they bombarded her with questions.

"Are you okay? What happened? How do you feel?"

"I've never felt better!" Deliah exclaimed. "I saw this

glorious green light, and then a beautiful fairy with curly blonde hair, draped in an exquisite gown of green velvet healed me. Her name was Elvina, and she said I was to come back and go to the hills of Nuverny, and she gave me this." Deliah reached in her dress pocket and pulled out a clear crystal wand. "Then I saw you guys!" Herbie let a tear slide down his cheek before wiping it away embarrassed.

Deliah looked around from wall to wall at this unbelievable crystal cave, seeing it for the first time.

"Wow! Thank you," she said quietly with deep appreciation for the crystals.

Bright lights shot toward the end of the cave, and there was a marvelous echo as if the cave were saying, "You're welcome."

The gnomes introduced themselves to Deliah, and she patted each of her rescuers on the head and shoulders. They led her toward the forest. When they arrived outside the cave, Deliah and Ostephen thanked the Greenland gnomes for their help. They brushed their feet on the grass and blushed bashfully.

"Aw, shucks! It's nothin'," Herbie said. "Deliah, let me see that crystal wand for a second, will ya?"

As Deliah handed it to Herbie, he wrapped it tightly in both hands and mumbled, "Greenland gnomes, where ya be? Greenland gnomes, I be needin' thee."

He held up the crystal, then handed it to Deliah. She stared at it in amazement.

"It's you! I can see you all in the crystal!" she exclaimed.

"That ya can," Herbie replied. "If you ever need us again, Dearie, you just hold that wand there and you'll know where we are. Just ask it for our help, and we'll come a runnin'."

"A runnin'!" they all echoed, nodding their heads affirmatively.

Deliah knelt down and kissed Herbie on the cheek. He turned deep red, kicked at the ground, and stuffed his hands in his pockets. She blew the rest of the Greenland gnomes a kiss and waved goodbye as Ostephen graciously bowed before them with respect.

Then the little blue fairy and the little brave girl journeyed onward and upward toward the hills of Nuverny.

Merlin   Maury

Chapter 8

Butterflies, dragonflies, birds all take flight.
The eagle soars through the clear, blue sky.
Close your eyes, lie back on the grass.
In the sun and beauty, you shall bask.

Nuverny was known as one of the most promising and glorious places in the realm. It was home to the Great Ones, the Wise Ones, and the Elderly. It was rumored that Merlin often made unexpected appearances there. Nuverny never had many visitors, as only old souls were even aware of it, and they must be greatly respected to be allowed entrance. The hills of Nuverny were plenty and very green. Even disrobed, they could easily qualify as one of the Seven Wonders of the World. Each high-reaching hill hovered above you. They were colossal and sky scraping. The Great Ones, Wise Ones, and Elderlys all sat atop their own hill and appropriately appeared that much closer to heaven.

It was evident that if someone made their way up the wrong hill, he would be quite tired by the time he got back down and found the correct one. Not sure exactly why Elvina had told her to go to Nuverny, Deliah decided to turn to the wand. Standing at the bottom of the hills of Nuverny, she pulled out her wand and silently asked what she should seek. The wand began to light up, and she quickly saw long, flowing grey hair under a pointy hat. A very tall man in a long, dark blue robe covered with silver stars was sitting atop a hill mixing potions.

"Thank you," Deliah said, putting the wand away.

"It's Merlin," Ostephen said in complete awe. "Deliah, this is such an honor. Merlin doesn't appear for just anyone. He only takes students who go through years of training. This means we are getting close. If you're ready for Merlin, you're....Well, you're just plain ready!"

"Whoo!" Deliah let out a deep breath, preparing to meet one of the greatest wizards of all time.

Ostephen flew up above the hills, buzzing left then right, scanning for a pointy hat. He flew back to Deliah.

"This way!" he exclaimed and headed left, then forward. "He is the last hill on the left side. He's making a potion," he said impressed.

Deliah and Ostephen reached the bottom of the hilltop and looked at each other frightfully. They both let out a long sigh.

Ostephen asked, "Ready for this?"

Deliah nodded, and placing one foot in front of the other, began to climb the steep hill. She looked at Ostephen hovering in front of her and trying to be encouraging, but all she could think was *I wish I had wings*.

She was nearly out of breath when she reached the top and heard a gentle yet powerful voice say, "Deliah, I've been expecting you. You're right on time."

There was a narrow cave, and Merlin stepped forward to the entrance and gestured them inside, the tip of his pointy hat grazing the top of the cave as he turned. Deliah and Ostephen followed him inside. The cave sparkled, and there were several dragonflies providing the light. She looked into Merlin's icy blue eyes, which you could almost see through, and felt overwhelmed by his presence, but she could still sense his friendliness. He handed her a vial and gestured for her to drink it. She gulped it down and was amazed at the sweet taste of it.

"It's like candy!"

Merlin laughed and said, "That will help energize you after the climb." He gestured to a large, colorful, spotted mushroom across from him and said, "Have a seat."

Deliah politely sat, and Ostephen settled into his usual front pocket of the cloak. He remained oddly quiet while he observed Merlin in awe.

"Well, dear child, you have done well, very well. I've been

59

watching you, and I'm here to prepare you for the next stage of this journey. You are about to encounter some very dangerous things. You need to be aware at all times."

Deliah's focus was suddenly broken when she felt a tickle on her ankle. Bending down to scratch her leg and fix her sock, she shrieked at the sight of two blue, smiling eyes and jumped up. Merlin gave a low chuckle.

"Maury doesn't like to be left out."

Deliah, who was now standing close beside Merlin for protection, was staring at the large mushroom in shock.

"Go on, Maury. Introduce yourself," Merlin said. "I'm almost finished mixing Deliah's potions." And with that, Merlin turned his back and continued filling several vials.

"Hi! I'm Maury, Maury the mushroom."

"Nice to meet you, Maury," Deliah said quietly.

In a very deep, low voice Maury slowly continued, "Merlin's been working *all* night long on your potions."

Deliah smiled. There was something about this mushroom. He was just so harmless and friendly that she instantly liked him.

"I'm sorry I sat on you," Deliah said.

"Oh, don't be," Maury replied in his slow drawl. "That's what I'm here for."

"You're the most colorful mushroom I've ever seen."

"Why, thank you," Maury replied. He was a bright orange mushroom with white spots and little blue eyes. "I help Merlin grow some of the herbs and oils he needs in his magic," Maury said proudly.

"Speaking of which," Merlin interjected, "I am done."

He closed the lid on a tiny wooden box full of vials filled with brightly colored liquids. One was a glowing, sparkling pink. It immediately caught Deliah's eye.

"Have a seat," Maury said, leaning the top of his mushroom cap in her direction.

Deliah gently sat atop Maury the mushroom, dangling her legs over the side. Now that she was aware that the mushroom had a face, she was much more comfortable.

Just when I thought I've seen it all, Deliah thought to herself.

"Indeed," Merlin said aloud, "there is a whole world just waiting to be discovered."

Deliah was taken aback. She was sure she hadn't said that out loud.

"Yes, I've learned a few things over the years, dear Deliah. Telepathic communication is just one of them," Merlin exclaimed. "It's more natural than speaking in fact, but like everything else in this realm, it will be awhile before that is uncovered by your kind."

"Wow!"

Deliah was impressed, but she was now extra careful to watch her thoughts. Merlin chuckled, sensing this.

"You see, Deliah, there are no secrets, no mysteries if man were just to trust in what he seeks," Merlin declared. His tall frame leaned over to put the box of potions in her hands. She looked at them, wondering what they were for. "These are healing potions. They will come in handy; you will know what you need." Winking oddly in Ostephen's direction, Merlin continued, "There is so much love to go around. There is so much light to be illuminated. Be the match to ignite the flame. For soon, there will be no igniting left, as only light shall remain."

Deliah stood before this very tall, very wise wizard and suddenly found herself speechless.

Saved by the mushroom, Maury interjected with a slow drawl of "Now, girl, you are to head north of Nuverny and through Tiki-Tal. Merlin's been giving you signs; you'll know where to go from there."

With a swish of Merlin's robe and a snap of his fingers, he produced a tiki torch and handed it to Deliah. With a knowing wink, he closed his eyes and vanished.

Ostephen led Deliah out to the mouth of the cave. She awkwardly half-climbed, half-ran back down the hill, Maury's words still echoing in her mind.

Snilly

Chapter 9

A deer, rabbit, fox, or bear;
A friend of Mother Nature to protect and care;
A raven, wolf, or dancing light—
There's always a guardian in the forest at night.

As they made their way into Tiki-Tal, Deliah felt it might be time to broach a certain subject with Ostephen. It was clear that Rosella had eyes for Ostephen, and she was curious to see if the feeling was mutual.

"So Rosella sure is nice," Deliah said.

"Oh, yes, she's wonderful," Ostephen agreed. "We've been dear friends ever since I can remember."

Clearly, Ostephen was blind to the adoration Rosella had for him, yet Deliah had easily picked up on it. She was sure everyone else in the realm had as well and was just waiting for Ostephen to wake up and see it for himself. Deliah was sure Rosella was right when she had said, "He loves me. He just doesn't know it yet." Ostephen carried on about Rosella's many remarkable qualities, and he didn't even flinch when he mentioned the many suitors she had. Somehow he was blind as to why Rosella never seemed interested in any of them.

"Perhaps she wasn't interested because she was feeling a little blue," Deliah joked.

"Hmm, perhaps," he replied completely unaware.

"You know, when we are done saving the kingdom and all, you should come back and perhaps enjoy a nice holiday together," Deliah urged. Deliah had liked Rosella the very first time she met her; Rosella was a content, beautifully simplistic fairy. She really did have love for Ostephen, and Deliah prayed he would realize it before it was too late.

Just then, a fairy dressed rather cupid-like shot an arrow into Ostephen's little blue behind.

"Ow!" he cried, pulling out the arrow, dropping it to the ground, and rubbing the assaulted cheek.

"The love fairy," Deliah said giggling with surprise before dashing off to find her.

They both looked around but didn't see anything or anyone. Ostephen assumed it was a practical joke.

"Very funny. That hurt! It was probably the bush people; they get bored and like to make me the butt of their jokes," Ostephen reasoned.

Realizing the humor in his own statement, they both fell over in laughter but quickly regained composure at the sound of an all-too-familiar buzz. Darting behind a tree, they watched as a slew of Dark Ones and Kahorgis stealthily crept by. They could hear the pack leader say, "We have to stop them before they reach you know what. If they reach it, we lose power and force, and the Dark King will be irate and unforgiving."

Ostephen and Deliah looked at each other and mouthed "Reach what?" in unison. As soon as the path was clear, they came out of the trees and continued on their trek.

Making their way to Tiki-Tal, Deliah couldn't help but ask, "Ostephen? What would you do if you never got to see Kristoff again, if you had in fact lost him forever?"

Ostephen looked into her big brown eyes and saw a lingering grief.

"I suppose part of me would be forever changed, forever missing. Nevertheless, I would meet each day anew and try to live life the way Kristoff would have wanted me to, the way he did, to the fullest."

A single tear escaped and slid down Deliah's cheek.

"Sometimes I feel so alone and so tired. I just want things to be the way they were when Papa was with me, the way they were supposed to be."

Ostephen sat on her shoulder and wiped away the tear, leaving a trail of blue sparkles behind it.

"Love has many forms, Deliah. They may not always last physically, but I can assure you that when one has experienced the kind of love you and I have experienced—you for your father and I for my brother—well, that love doesn't just vanish. It remains the same; it just changes form, I suppose."

"Yeah, I suppose. It's strange, but I feel closer to Papa being on this journey than I have in months."

"Everything is exactly as it should be," Ostephen said.

Deliah thought he might be right.

• • •

Snilly the snail swooshed along ever so slowly. Deliah watched, wondering if he were indeed moving at all.

"So, you see," he said, "Tiki-Tal is one of the warmest and most relaxing places to live."

Ostephen began yawning again; this snail was putting him to sleep.

"Look, Snilly," he said not at all surprised that Snilly's Tiki-Tal tour business venture had backfired, "can you please just point us in some kind of direction?"

Snilly sighed and embarked on another lecture, "Well, define direction. I mean, direction can be perceived...."

Ostephen rolled his eyes, looked at Deliah in desperation, and asked, "Have you received any signs? Anything from Merlin?"

"No, I can't think of anything."

Deliah wracked her brain. Frustrated, she hated that she was supposed to know something and had no idea what it was. She wanted to prove that she had what it takes to fulfill the prophecy. She felt like she needed to prove it to herself.

"It's okay. Don't worry. We'll figure it out when the time is right," Ostephen assured her, trying to ease her tension. "Sometimes when you stop thinking about something, it has a tendency to appear. That's why fairies never stress. We just play and forget our worries, knowing that eventually everything comes about."

She gave him a small smile, admiring his positive attitude.

Snilly slowly slid alongside them. Unable to keep up, Snilly eventually waved goodbye and asked them to come back for a full free tour of Tiki-Tal when they had the time. He was still talking as they walked off into the distance.

"I think Snilly is sweet," Deliah remarked.

Ostephen grimaced. "Well, we know where to go if we ever have trouble sleeping," he retorted, faking a loud snore. They giggled and began humming Papa's favorite Irish tune as they skipped onward down the bend.

Chapter 10

The sun radiates warmth and light as does your smile.
A smile has the power to transform a life.
A good deed, such as a hug, is a tiny gesture,
But it creates little sparks of divine light
That glow like fairies and spread like wildflowers.

They didn't get very far around the bend before Deliah stopped.

"Ostephen, something feels weird. The last few days I've had an uncomfortable feeling like we were being watched."

Just then there was a rustling in the bushes, and she turned to see a Kahorgi-like foot slip beneath the bush.

"We *are* being watched, Deliah. The Dark King has Kahorgis stationed throughout the land. Your feeling is increasing because we are getting closer. I'm sure he didn't think you'd make it this far, so he is stepping up his defenses," Ostephen whispered.

Deliah rubbed her stomach, feeling sick from all the nervous energy. Ostephen pointed to a small cave and suggested that they take a short break. Deliah welcomed anything that would stop her mind from reeling. While munching on fruit and staring into the fire they'd made using their tiki torch, Deliah remembered to tell Ostephen about a recurring vision she'd been having in her dreams.

"I keep seeing a rainbow," she said.

Ostephen lit up and shouted, "Of course! Rainbow's Pass! That's the sign Merlin's been sending you! Why didn't I think of it? We must get to Rainbow's Pass at once!"

He snuffed out the fire at once and waved Deliah onto the path. She grabbed her torch and hurriedly followed her little blue friend.

"Rainbow's Pass only shines but once a year," he explained urgently. "If we can connect with the rainbow before it disappears, we will have secured our trail from the Dark Ones for a solid twenty-two hours. This is the time we need to gather the entire realm and prepare before we reach Dark Corner."

"Where the Dark King resides," Deliah confirmed nervously.

"Yes, it's critical that we have the twenty two hours to gather with our realm without being seen."

"How much farther to the rainbow?" Deliah asked. "Oh, dear!" she said in surprise as the crystal wand in her pocket began to shake and rattle. Looking into the wand, she saw Herbie. He had a message for them.

"Laflin asked me to contact you both. Congratulations on receiving the sign! He and the missus have been to Rainbow's Pass. The rainbow is already opened; you have less than three hours before it'll begin to fade. Ask Snilly for directions. He'll know how to reach it fastest, and he's great with calculations."

The wand then flashed, showing them Snilly still sleeping soundly a few yards back, so they quickly turned and ran. Out of breath and with flushed cheeks, Ostephen knocked on Snilly's smooth burgundy shell, and Snilly slowly slipped his head out and yawned.

"Well, hello again, my friends."

"Snilly, we need your help. What is the fastest way to connect with Rainbow's Pass?"

Snilly pulled a Tiki-Tal tour brochure out of nowhere.

"Ah! Rainbow's Pass, you say? Well, given the dimension and time of year…taking into consideration the weather and land mass…."

"Snilly, please!" Ostephen sputtered. "We must hurry!"

"Veer left and run. You are a few miles off; however, being in Tiki-Tal, you are closer than most other places. If you keep your pace, you will arrive in two hours, twenty-two minutes, and two seconds."

"Very well! Thanks!" they shouted as they ran off.

"What's the rush?" Snilly sighed. "There's plenty of time." And with that, he yawned and retreated back into his shell for another nap.

It began to rain heavily. Ostephen, completely focused, continued to fly hard. Deliah's pace slowed slightly as she struggled with her cloak, trying to shield herself from the downpour. Ostephen looked back and saw her struggle and began to laugh.

"What?" Deliah asked, seeing the look he gave her.

"Nothing. It's just your human side shining through," he teased. "We fairies see the rain for the gift it is."

He playfully flew down to splash in a puddle. Shaking his wings, droplets flew everywhere, and he threw back his head, letting the rain fall across his face.

Deliah watched and admired his zeal. She realized that she had it all wrong. She let her cloak fall off her head, splashed in a puddle, and felt free as the rain splattered across her face, drops landing on her tongue and sitting on her lashes. They both started laughing and enjoying the childlike abandon that fairies embrace and live so well.

They ran on, laughing and splashing all the way through the storm. The fun energy acted like an invisible force, pushing them forward even faster. When the sun reappeared, Deliah could see the rainbow in the distance. The majestic stretch of color shined across the land with its vibrant hues casting an arch of unspeakable beauty. Deliah noticed a group of butterflies fluttering alongside them and felt encouraged, so she removed her shoes and ran faster. Moments later, they reached the foot of Rainbow's Pass, and the butterflies hovered directly in front of them, signaling that they had made it.

"They're all waiting on the other side. You may pass. Go on," the butterflies urged them.

Ostephen and Deliah walked through the rainbow's fine veil of mist and came out at Rainbow's End to find all their friends waiting to meet them. The entire elemental kingdom had gathered to help. Deliah stood awestruck.

Merlin came forward, put his hand on her shoulder, and whispered, "Believe indeed. Believe you do, for when you believe, life unfolds to you."

With an outstretched arm, he gestured across the valley

full of elementals before taking a seat with Maury, who dipped his mushroom cap in acknowledgment of her. Her heart was pounding, and her eyes were tearing up because she had never seen so many gather for a cause with so much unity and so much love.

Deliah assumed there would be talk of a great battle, and she stood ready to hear the plans of how they would fight, how they would conquer all, and how victory would be claimed. But as she looked from one beautiful creature of the earth to another, she saw no traces of fear, no anger, no bitterness. She saw and felt only love. There were no battle plans or sneaky attacks to plot; there were only creatures immersed in pure love.

One by one, the fairies, gnomes, unicorns, foxes, dragonflies, frogs, trees, and all the friends of the kingdom stepped forward into a circle. Ostephen sat on her shoulder, and he was the last to step forward. One by one, all the creatures slowly closed their eyes and began to pray silently. Deliah glanced around at the circle full of thousands of lights—all shining, all trusting, all loving.

"This must be what magic feels like," Deliah said to herself as she closed her eyes.

She began to pray for Papa, for her friends, for Faye; soon she could swear she felt her heart open. It was as if someone had taken a key and unlocked it. She wasn't sure where she was or what created this enveloping divine energy; she only knew that she never wanted it to leave. It never occurred to Deliah that a battle could be fought with prayer or love for that matter.

It was then that she saw Papa appear, and she heard him say, "What is won with war? It is more appropriate to ask what is lost? No matter what the situation, turn to love. If you ever feel lost or attacked, you will not find justice or resolution in fighting back. No, you will find it in love. For those who have ill intentions toward you, love them deeply."

Papa disappeared, and the circle remained intact for hours as they spread their message and united their power. Deliah practiced the gift of foresight, which the elementals had taught her in Greenland. She almost felt as though she was out of her body and looking down on the whole experience. She knew that no matter how bad things got, she could come back to this moment and find this sense of security.

Slowly, one by one, someone would bow or give a token of blessing to the center of the circle and then leave. Eventually, only Deliah, Ostephen, and Merlin remained. Merlin waved his hand over all the gifted blessings, which included feathers, coins, flowers, letters, necklaces, pictures, fairy dust, and more. As he did so, the items transformed into snow-white doves that flew into the sky above and formed the shape of a heart. Deliah and Ostephen looked on in awe before bowing before Merlin whose form instantly shifted into an eagle. As an eagle, Merlin led the doves as they flew east. Deliah and Ostephen sat together in silence, unable to move, unwilling to let the experience go.

Deliah felt like she had gained a whole new perspective. She felt safer knowing she could control her fear to a certain extent, slow her breathing, and find concentration when she needed it. Rainbow's Pass had taught her to trust her feelings and to focus on what she wanted to have happen instead of believing everything was beyond her control.

It had been a day since Rainbow's End, and Deliah and Ostephen had continued on their journey, following a flock of white doves for the better part of the day when they heard a low chant and moved in its direction. They were curious what it may be.

Dark King
Kahorgi Dark Ones

Chapter 11

Come one, come all when the fairies call.
Forget all your worries, troubles, and cares.
Dance in the forest with the bears.
See that tiny sparkling light?
'Tis your fairy guiding you through the night.

Deliah turned to see a wild-looking creature with an abundance of messy, twig-like hair; a large nose; and a grass skirt.

"Good heavens!" she said to Ostephen, "What on earth was that?"

"Shh!" Ostephen whispered. "They're forest Nimbles. Listen closely, and you'll hear their song."

They both fell silent. Sure enough, as the Nimbles danced around a ring of fire, Deliah heard a low chant.

"Nimblee-ee-ee. Nimblee-oo-oo. Ee-ee-ee-ee. Oo-oo-oo-oo."

They were casting their hands in unison toward the fire, causing it to grow larger and larger with each movement. They were stomping loudly and moving in a clockwise circle. Their medium-sized bodies were pale in comparison to their outlandish hair.

"Strange things the Nimbles are," Ostephen said with a shrug.

"Should we maybe approach them and say hello?" Deliah wondered.

"No! You don't talk to a Nimble unless invited, and you

don't question a Nimble either. Those are the rules."

Just then, the Nimbles all grew silent as their flame reached its highest point; inside the flame, they shared a vision of a little girl.

Deliah stepped on a twig, which made an inconvenient snapping sound. The Nimbles stopped and turned. When they recognized her as the girl from the fire, they sent their chief to invite her to join their ceremony. Intimidated yet intrigued, Deliah agreed, much to Ostephen's dismay.

As she followed the chief to the fire ring, he said, "We honor you."

"Oh, that's not necessary. Really, I'm just...."

Deliah was cut off by the chief who didn't look impressed. "We honor you," he said again. "You open arms to receive honor. Yes?"

"Yes?" Deliah said, smiling nervously, opening her arms wide. Ostephen sat beside her and—after receiving a few nudges—did the same, smirking all the while. At first she felt a little silly, but as the Nimbles continued their chant, she felt a wave of energy envelop her, and she felt amazingly powerful yet remarkably humble. She was really enjoying this experience.

"Nimblee-ee-ee. Nimblee-oo-oo."

She snuck a peek to the side and smiled when she saw Ostephen chanting "Ee-ee-ee-ee. Oo-oo-oo-oo" along with them. After the fire dance ended, the Nimbles bowed graciously before Deliah. All raised their hands toward the fire, which revealed another vision.

"You go here," Chief Nimble said. Deliah looked into the fire and saw a rocky terrain very close to the water. "Waverly Water's Edge," Chief Nimble explained. "You go. Must hurry. Must save."

Deliah thanked the Nimbles, and they all stood stomping and chanting as they urged her on.

"Nimblee-ee-ee. Nimblee-oo-oo."

Chapter 12

A fairy will dance; a fairy will play.
A fairy will find the joy in each day.
A laugh, a smile, a giggle or two.
Call on a fairy if you're feeling blue.

"What's one little fairy going to do? Leave him be!" they shouted and laughed as the Dark Ones tossed him aimlessly aside to lie weak and hidden among the jagged rocks.

"The tide will soon wash him away! Leave him to his death!" a Kahorgi shouted as they all guffawed and charged on.

• • •

The bewitching black raven soared through the sky seeking Ostephen and Deliah with the utmost urgency. He couldn't believe what he had just seen: Kristoff being cast aside by the Dark Ones! He knew Kristoff didn't have much time and was set on finding Deliah and Ostephen for his survival. Several other birds had heard his call for help and were in turn guiding the raven to Deliah and Ostephen's location. He was gaining hope that he would find them in time when he felt an intense pain in his right wing. He flapped even faster to keep from falling to the ground. His right wing was ablaze with flames; his fabulous feathers were on fire.

The Dark Ones laughed, "Try and find them now! What's the matter, raven? Can't fly? Fireball got ya? Stupid bird!"

The raven lay on the ground helpless and fighting for his life. He hung on despite the pain, knowing his friend's life depended on it.

• • •

The water crashed against the surface of the rocky shore with a force no one cared to challenge. It became apparent to Deliah that the closer to the Dark Corner they got, the more beauty seemed to be lost. The rocks were jagged and plenty, so you had to tread very carefully.

"I sure wish I could fly right now," Deliah said to Ostephen.

They had reached Waverly Water's Edge, but they still weren't sure why the Nimbles had sent them there. They'd been traveling awhile now with no sightings or information. The land seemed cold and eerily quiet.

What waited in Waverly? The question bounced back and forth in Deliah's mind.

Ostephen decided to lighten up the mood and began whistling a fairy song he'd been teaching her. Deliah smiled appreciatively and began humming along. They wandered up and down the rocky terrain, singing merrily as they went. Suddenly she saw a beautiful black raven with a broken wing, and she stopped in horror. A single tear rolled down her cheek at the sight of this ravishing raven in pain.

"Is there anything I can do?"

"Deliah," the bird said wearily, "I've been looking for you." His little eyes fluttered up and down, fighting to stay open. "The Dark Ones let Kristoff go, but they left him on the rocks at water's edge to die. You must help him; he is weakened from their spell. If someone doesn't find him, the tide will rise, and Kristoff will die."

The bird slowly succumbed and closed his eyes. Grateful that he was willing to risk his life for a friend, Deliah said a prayer for him. Then she ran to the water's edge where Ostephen had been visiting with the sea sprites.

"Ostephen! Ostephen!" she shouted.

By the time she reached the water's edge, she was completely out of breath and desperate to deliver the news. Exasperated, she grabbed the wand and yelled, "Show him!" The wand flashed to Kristoff who was miles away, lying hidden in the rocks at water's edge, weak and lifeless. "He's free, but he hasn't got much time," she managed.

Ostephen was speechless and started to fly off at once, but

she stopped him.

"We won't make it on foot."

She closed her eyes and with all the intention she could muster, called on Edwin. Deliah and Ostephen looked around but failed to see him. Suddenly, a pure white unicorn with a rose crest on his head rose out from the trees and skidded to a halt beside them. They jumped on, and without question, Edwin dashed off.

Ostephen was an absolute wreck, wringing his hands in desperation to get there.

"Why would they free him? Is it a trap? Maybe Kristoff's good determination and will proved too strong for them, and as the spell began to weaken, he remembered his truth and began to rebel against them?"

• • •

They reached the water's edge and searched desperately among the rocks. Ostephen could see a dim yellow light fading in and out, fighting hard for survival.

"Kristoff! Kristoff!" he shouted as he wrapped his arms around his brother's weak body.

Kristoff blinked, trying to regain clear vision. Upon making out the face, he mumbled bleakly, "Oste—" before his eyes closed. His body went limp. Ostephen buried his face in his brother's chest and sobbed.

"Noooo! Noooo!" he screamed. "Hold on! Hold on!"

Deliah was fighting back tears, trying to maintain a brave face for Ostephen. Except for the crashing of the unforgiving waves against the boulders and rocks, everything was silent. Deliah could see tears streaming down Ostephen's face. She made her way over to him and reached out a hand to comfort him, but he brushed it away despondent.

Suddenly inspired, Deliah reached into her cloak and grabbed the box of Merlin's potions. The pink potion was glowing brightly. She parted Kristoff's lips and gently poured the vile of it into his mouth, then sat in uncomfortable silence for what seemed like ages.

A pink light began to glow around his chest and then, like an arrow, Kristoff's body abruptly shot out of Ostephen's arms, went high into the sky, and disappeared. A few moments later, a bright yellow glow filled the area as he slowly came back down and hovered in front of them.

Ostephen was astonished. He flew up to meet the little yellow fairy. Looking into his eyes, he said, "It's you!" They glowed and buzzed happily around in circles and kept embracing each other.

"I'm sorry," Kristoff said, "I just wasn't myself. I would never...."

"I know. We all know." Then Ostephen remembered Deliah and said, "I'd like you to meet my dearest friend, Deliah."

Kristoff kissed her on the cheek, and the three began to sing and dance and had a little fairy party right there. Even Edwin joined in and neighed in joyful delight, adding a brilliant sparkle with his rose crest and horn.

• • •

The Dark King looked deep into his goblet and saw the three fairies reunited and joyful.

"What's this?" he screamed. "What's this madness?"

The gathered Kahorgis and Dark Ones standing nearby stumbled in front of the king.

One of them stammered, "Well, the spell was wearing off, you see, and he wasn't a harm. I mean, he was just one little fairy. Besides, we didn't think anyone would find him." The other Kahorgis all laughed.

The Dark King threw the goblet to the floor, splattering its dark, murky contents across their faces.

"No one! And I mean no one is to be released! Do you understand?"

"Uh, yes, sir. Yes, sir," they all mumbled apologetically.

The Dark King let out an unmerciful bellow, "Fools! Fools you are! You will stand guard out front because that is all you're capable of! Go!"

They retreated and stood by the main doors, shivering in the brisk night air. The Dark King sat back down.

"They do have a point. What is one teensy weensy fairy going to do? Blast it! It's nothing." He glared at a nearby Dark One and shouted, "Don't just stand there, fool! Get me a new drink!"

"Yes, sir!" the Dark One replied and buzzed off at once, a small trail of flames in his wake.

Chapter 13

The fairy folk, us fairy folk.
We laugh at the humans who think we're a joke.
For we are real, so real you see.
See us as we flit from tree to tree.

B eing reunited with his brother had brought about a strength in Ostephen that Deliah hadn't yet seen. He was energized; he was hopeful; he believed in the power of miracles because he had just experienced one. There was no doubt in his mind that the light would triumph. They had made it to Rainbow's Pass, and they had prepared as a kingdom for the ensuing battle. It was only a matter of weeks before they would reach the Dark Corner. All would be revealed; an end would be seen.

Deliah sat alone, gathering her thoughts and her own strength. She remembered something Papa would say whenever she would hear a story of a bad guy or a monster and get frightened. He would always hug her and say, "One light will always overpower any darkness. One light is all it takes. Just shine."

"Papa," Deliah said aloud, "please give me strength. I have a lot of people counting on me, and I don't want to let anyone down. I refuse. I owe it to Faye. I owe it to my home."

Papa appeared as a vision before her, and he said, "My sweet child, the light shines down, shines out, shines through. You've nothing to fear. Just be you."

His words comforted her greatly, and her worries eased. Something inside her shifted from nervousness to determination.

"I'm ready for you," she said. "I'm ready."

• • •

The Dark King laughed as he heard the little girl's words echo through his castle.

"Muahaha," he roared as he gripped the sides of his throne so tightly that he tore the arms off. He tossed them to the ground.

Through scathing teeth, he said, "We'll see! We'll see!"

Raising his hands, he sent waves of lightning crashing through the Dark Kingdom, and all its inhabitants guffawed proudly as several trees split in two, caught on fire, and fell to the ground sizzling, leaving nothing but a trail of black soot in their place.

• • •

Sitting by the shore, Ostephen was filling Kristoff in on the events of the journey and was enjoying a few moments of rest when a giant sea turtle swam up to them.

"Hello, Duin. The sea sprites told me you popped in for a visit. Sorry I missed you earlier."

"That's all right," Duin replied, putting a giant flipper on a rock to get a tad closer to them. Several sea sprites jumped up playfully next to him, splashing in the surf.

"Is that a sea sprite?" Deliah asked as she peered out. "They haven't any wings! They're so light!" A couple sea sprites waved to her and pretended they were surfing among the sea spray, while another was riding a seahorse.

"They're actually the other reason I came to speak with you," Duin said in his highly intelligent yet leisurely, professor-like drawl. "The sea sprites have received word from Dedrik the dragon that you should head to Mount Finity, home of the dragons. Dedrik has a gift for you, but I must warn you that Mount Finity is quite a trek, and you may tire easily."

"No worries," Edwin said, "I plan on sticking around this time. They need to conserve their energy, and a little extra protection couldn't hurt either."

"Very well," Duin said.

The sea sprites waved and invited them into the water, shouting "Come on in, it's fun!"

As Duin slowly slipped back into the water, he asked if

Deliah wanted to come along for a ride with him. She grabbed on to his shell; the others jumped in as well. They all splashed playfully, forgetting for a short while about any worries. A starfish landed on Deliah's forehead and peeked over her brow, bending a tentacle to say hello. Deliah giggled and floated on her back, enjoying the warmth of the sun on her face. Duin floated alongside her peacefully.

"I think you'll find Dedrik and the dragons quite useful."

"I'm not sure I care to see any dragons," Deliah said slightly terrified.

Duin noticed Deliah's hesitation and added, "Dragons tend to get portrayed as dark or dangerous, but they can serve as guides just like fairies or angels. Dedrik has much to offer. She is a wise one. She is the guardian of treasures and of hidden wisdom."

After a calm hour spent basking in the afternoon sun with the sea folk, they collected their belongings, hopped on Edwin's back, and took off for Mount Finity.

Dedrik

Chapter 14

Spread the love, spread the joy, and
Rejoice in the glory of the land.
Nature, oh nature,
Truly man's best friend.

The white, snow-capped mountaintops were a far cry from the forest greenery and waters they had just traversed. They were thankful for Edwin; he had carried them such a distance and saved them so much time. They searched for Dedrik in every area she was known to be but failed to find her. A bird-like squawk filled the air, and they nearly tripped over one another as an enormous red dragon landed in front of them on the mountaintop. Her red scales glittered, and her eyelashes gleamed gold.

"You have traveled far and shown great tenacity," the dragon began. "You have awoken the primal energies within you and therefore around you. There is a hidden treasure on Mount Finity; I wish to share it with you."

The dragon shuffled back as she unfolded and lifted her right wing, revealing a large red ruby.

"This gem is a window into the Dark Corner. It will reveal to you the location of the Dark Ones as well as the Dark King's intentions. This ruby was once in the hands of the Dark Ones, but the Wise Ones and Elderlys found it and blessed it so that it could only be used by those with pure intentions. The Wise Ones and Elderlys then left it with the dragons, fierce protectors whom the Dark Ones tend to shy away from."

The dragon reached out a talon and dropped the ruby in Deliah's hands. The ruby glowed and flashed, and they could see the Dark King casting a black cloud with lightning across the land. The gem flashed again, and they saw the Kahorgis and the Dark Ones in combat training.

Dedrik locked eyes with Deliah and said, "The absence of fear is where power lies. Do not be fooled by the Dark King, for he has much fear. His castle and his very existence are built upon it. There is nothing sacred about that. Know that the dragons are with you."

Deliah suddenly felt a strong presence around her. She looked up to see a dragon perched on every mountaintop within eyesight.

"You have integrity, support, and love. You can persevere, my child," Dedrik concluded.

Kristoff had been holding his hand up periodically, wings flapping urgently, trying to get Dedrik's attention.

"Yes, Kristoff?" Dedrik asked at last.

"Are you a fire-breathing dragon?" he asked, his eyes growing in excitement.

"Yes," Dedrik replied, batting her golden lashes.

Kristoff clasped his yellow hands together and begged, "Pretty please!"

Ostephen joined in, asking "Just a wee one?"

Dedrik laughed and flew above the mountaintop as though she were about to leave. A small snort of smoke left her nostrils. Kristoff and Ostephen mumbled disheartened, and then they saw a huge flame as Dedrik turned to the side and released a large breath of fire. The flames took the shape of Pan dancing and playing his flute. He leaned forward in the flame as if he were playing a special note just for them.

Dedrik yelled, "Looks like you're headed for Piper's Point!"

She winked and departed, the other dragons following.

"Sweet!" Kristoff and Ostephen said in unison, watching Pan and the flame vanish into a thin puff of smoke before fading into the sky.

Chapter 15

Unicorns, leprechauns, magicians—it's true.
Fantasies, myths—call them what you will,
But these are reality; you know this still.

As the foursome neared Piper's Point, they were surrounded by sheep and livestock.

"Where to now?" asked Kristoff.

They looked at one another with uncertainty, and then the sound of melodic music began to rise.

"I think that's a flute. Perhaps Pan is leading us to him," Deliah said. Edwin carried them onward toward the music where they saw Pan, half-goat and half-man, sitting on a tree trunk, playing to an attentive audience of big horn sheep. He continued to play as he walked toward them, the sheep parting to let him through, and eventually he stopped before them.

His music slowly came to an end, and he tucked his flute away.

"Pleasure!" he said cheerily.

"Pan, is it?" Deliah asked, extending her hand.

He nodded, ignored Deliah's extended hand, and gave her a hearty hug.

"Pan, indeed. I reckon I drew you four in just as I did the sheep!" he said with a chuckle.

"Your music is enchanting," Deliah agreed.

"Ah, thank ya, miss. Music is truly healing, I believe. Never fails to calm my soul or ignite inspiration."

Pan was direct, and he always made eye contact. He was

quite a commanding presence to be around, yet he was gentle and unassuming at the same time.

He looked at Deliah's feet and said, "You must be tired. I reckon ya should trade those in for a pair of these" and pointed to his hooves. She giggled, staring at his hooves. "Well, my dear, shall we get you and your friends the information?"

"Information?" they all echoed.

"Ya didn't stumble upon Piper's Point for nothin'. Me playing that song was no coincidence. It's a bit of an omen, it is. Songs about Valley Low," he said, walking and waving them onto a nearby ledge of land. Standing on the dry rock, they all looked down. "That's Valley Low," Pan said as he pointed down to the never-ending brown rock.

"I think I'd prefer Valley High," Deliah mumbled.

"So ya ready?" Pan asked.

"Ready for what?" Deliah asked fearfully, as she already knew the answer.

"Why, to journey below, of course," Pan replied.

A large piece of rock crumbled under Edwin's weight and started to move, and he shuffled back onto his hind hooves. His horn started to glow as another piece of rock gave way and fell to the valley below. Edwin struggled not to fall with it. Several of the big horn sheep got closer to the edge and formed a wall around Edwin. They were used to rock climbing and didn't waste any time in an emergency. He managed to save himself, and they all breathed a sigh of relief as they watched the brown rock tumble and break as it bounced off the rock walls before crumbling to pieces below.

"That's why there's only one way into Valley Low," Pan said. They all looked at him ridden with anxiety. "The underground tunnels," he continued.

"Follow me!" he shouted. He pulled out his flute and began to play the same melody. He guided them a few miles up the mountain where they came to a tiny wooden barn. He pushed through the doors and shouted, "In here, lads!"

One by one, they walked through the barn doors and found themselves instantly transported underground to a dry, dark hole. Pan took a candle off a hook near the door, struck a match on his hoof, and lit it. He then shoved the candle into the end of his flute, creating a makeshift lantern. Kristoff and Ostephen provided a slight glow, and Edwin's horn lit up quite a bit; between these two light sources, the path through the tunnel was passable.

"Now I'll warn ya. Valley Low is where the gray exist. The gray are those who don't want to play a part in favoring the light or the dark. They dwell in Valley Low and gladly go unnoticed. So if you see a shadow, don't be affright. Their favorite time to come out is night."

Kristoff and Ostephen locked eyes and together moved closer to Pan.

"So what is this omen? The song you were playing?" Deliah asked.

"Ah, yes, miss. It's the omen of the light." The song began to sound from his flute even though he was not playing it as he spoke. "The omen was written long ago that a girl will one day appear. A girl with wings and hair of the earth, a girl so sad and forlorn. She will awaken and seek her truth. At once, the blueprint is born." Deliah rubbed her arms as she felt a chill, and several goosebumps formed. "The realm will gather, and all will be one, intent to eradicate fear. Through the Valley Low she will go and save him as he lies asleep. King Finvarra shall be set free as by her, the prophecy."

"Finvarra!" Ostephen and Kristoff shouted. "Finvarra, Fin Fin Faye!" they chanted three times over with Pan and Edwin.

Pan's music and lyric stopped as he looked them all in the eye and said, "Finvarra shall be set free."

Deliah, sorry to break up their circle of excitement, asked, "Pan, does the omen say exactly how the girl goes about doing this?"

Pan, quiet and serious for a moment, replied, "The twisted root lies hidden in the heart of Valley Low where Finvarra sleeps inside. The only way to open it is to find the twisted root key."

"Twiglet!" Ostephen and Kristoff shouted. "I heard a story once that he may have come close to finding it, but his family denied it."

"Who's Twiglet?" Deliah asked.

"Twiglet was born of the Twiggen family. They helped out at the baby pine nursery, you see. Mrs. Twiggen likes to be involved and keep busy. Twiglet, well, he can be a wild little guy. Some

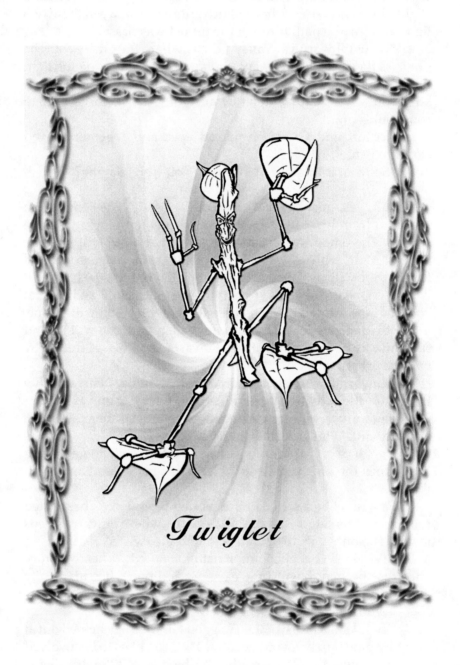

Twiglet

can't decide whether he's a creative genius or just plain crazy. I've always liked Twiglet myself," Ostephen said.

"He's certainly not boring," Kristoff added.

And so, they decided that when they reached the end of the tunnel, they would set out for the baby pine nursery, which wasn't far from Valley Low.

Pan continued to lead the group when he suddenly blew out the candle and in a hushed voice instructed them all to huddle close against the wall. The four of them stood in alarmed silence against the dry, dirty wall of the cave.

"It's a gray. Be quiet and still," Pan whispered.

Deliah held her breath in fear as a shadowy gray figure slowly drifted closer toward them. Kristoff and Ostephen stood stark still, their eyes bugging out of their heads. They all felt a cold chill as if they had suddenly gotten caught in a winter storm. The gray seemed to almost stop; it moved at an even slower pace as it moved alongside them. It paused and seemed to be looking right at them. Deliah had never been so grateful for the dark. They all prayed silently that it would pass.

Just let it pass, they pleaded over and over in their minds.

The gray gave off a low moan. Deliah desperately wanted to cover her ears but was too frightened to move for fear the gray would hear her. Moments later, the gray began to drift forward again. Just when they thought they might breathe a sigh of relief, two more followed in its wake. Deliah closed her eyes; she couldn't bear to look at the grays. They were scarier than any nightmare she'd ever had. They were so dark and hollow-looking, just shadows devoid of any real feeling.

Several minutes later, Edwin assured them that the grays were all gone. Pan struck another match and relit the candle.

"I don't know if I can do this," Deliah said, breathing a monstrous sigh. "That was close, too close."

"Come on, carry on. We're nearing the end. No choice but to go forward now," Pan replied.

He gestured for her to walk closer to him, and with another large sigh, they continued to creep through the tunnel, more alert than ever. It had felt much longer than it actually took to reach the end of the tunnel and come out into Valley Low. In the center, they saw the twisted root. It was hard to imagine something as grand as a king lying hidden in the heart of it.

"Well, we're here, but all is useless without the key," Pan declared.

"Edwin, can you take us out of Valley Low and to the baby pine nursery a few miles ahead?" the brothers asked.

Edwin nodded, and they all gathered round him and closed their eyes. Upon opening them, they found temporary relief of the dry dirt that covered Valley Low.

Chapter 16

Intrigue, curiosity, wonder — why?
For we are the joy you miss as a child.
Be five again, why not?
You've every right to enjoy your lot.

The smell of pine trees filled the air, and they all breathed in its heavenly scent. Ostephen said hello to all the baby pines, knowing that one day they would be transported to his favorite place: the forest of pines. They followed a voice singing nursery rhymes. Sure enough, it was Mrs. Twiggen singing the baby pines to sleep as she tended to them. Slowly, bark-covered lids began to fall until the entire nursery of baby pines was sleeping soundly. Mrs. Twiggen was dusting her thin hands of twig on her apron when she spotted the five of them heading toward her. Waving her little wooden limbs, she quickly motioned them to the left where they wouldn't disrupt her sleeping babies.

"Lookin' good, Mrs. Twiggen!" Ostephen said as he gestured to the nursery.

Mrs. Twiggen bowed her head slightly with graciousness.

"I'm so glad I chose to come here. It was the right thing to do, although Twiglet wouldn't agree," Mrs. Twiggen confessed. She extended her wooden limb to Deliah, saying "Pleasure to meet you. I've heard of your journey, and I'm grateful you accepted your mission." Deliah carefully shook Mrs. Twiggen's hand and smiled back warmly.

"Speaking of Twiglet," Kristoff said as they all looked around, suddenly wondering where Pan had gone. They saw him

91

off in the distance playing a quiet melody to the nursery.

Picking up on his brother's lead, Ostephen decided to get straight to it.

"Mrs. Twiggen, we need your help with the twisted root key."

"No, No. I know nothing. It was all Twiglet. He was messing around one day, and when he tried to tell his father and me, we assured him that we wanted nothing to do with it. Nothing. I had grays haunting this nursery day and night for weeks after. Luckily, these pines are strong." She shook her head, growing frustrated with the memory.

"I understand," Edwin assured her. "Do you think you could help us find Twiglet?"

"Your guess is as good as mine, I'm sure," she replied hastily. "That boy...."

Two baby pines started fussing, and she rushed off to tend to them, a few tiny leaves rustling on her little twig legs as she went.

"I have an idea," Deliah said, gripping the mermaid's bracelet. "Show me Twiglet," she commanded.

She suddenly had a clear vision of Twiglet who was in trouble—as usual. They all gasped when Deliah explained that she saw him in Valley Low caught between two Dark Ones and a Kahorgi who were teasing and taunting and trying to turn him to their side.

Kristoff, knowing all too well what Twiglet was dealing with, shouted, "Let's go! We have to help him!"

It seemed they'd lost Pan for good, his music still an echo throughout the nursery. The remaining three hopped on top of Edwin, and he magically transported them to Twiglet who was just over the hill from the pine nursery.

• • •

"Come on, Twig. You know you're better than the rest. Don't let them hold you back. Be a star. Show them."

The Dark Ones showed Twiglet a vision of a mansion. It was a long held desire of Twiglet's to own a mansion where he could throw the best parties in all of Faye. The vision vanished, and Twiglet snapped back to reality when he heard the voices of two old friends.

"Twiglet! No!" Kristoff and Ostephen buzzed over and took hold of Twiglet, but the Dark Ones started throwing fire, trying to burn him. The fairies made their glow brighter in hopes of blinding the Dark Ones, and Deliah used her crystal wand to try and block them.

The Dark Ones recognized Kristoff and took aim at him with fireballs.

"So you didn't die, huh, yellow? Well, don't worry. We'll finish what we started. Muahaha!"

Deliah pointed the light from the wand in their direction and the two vanished.

Regaining his sense of self, Twiglet hugged his dear friends. He said, "Thank you" over and over again as his eyes welled up.

"You've gotta get a grip, Twiglet. These Dark Ones are no joke. A second too late and, well, you might have been captive in the Dark Corner. You know, your mom may be right; sometimes it doesn't hurt to play it safe," Kristoff said gently.

After catching up and introducing Deliah to Twiglet, Ostephen got to the heart of the matter.

"We need to find the twisted root key, Twiglet," Ostephen declared. "We need to set our king free."

Shadows of grays appeared in Twiglet's eyes.

"I've never actually seen it," he said, "but I've come close. Okay, I will do what I can. After all, you just saved me."

Deliah found it hard to believe that Twiglet could get into so much trouble. He was so little; his twig legs and arms were so tiny. It was certainly a displaced sense of adventure, she decided.

"It's buried by the actual tree, but it's guarded so well that it's nearly impossible to get close," Twiglet began as he recalled the day he found the key's location. "As usual, I was bored so I was looking round for…something. Mom had warned me about Valley Low, but she never told me about the grays or its real dangers. I decided to hike down, but when I wanted to turn back, the shadows kept leading me in deeper and deeper. I was getting close to the tree when the grays came upon me, and I was so scared that I fell to the ground and played dead—a twig's best defense. It worked; they couldn't track my energy. As I lay there, I heard the key. Being a twig, I could hear the key calling to me. The root that was used to make the key and the tree itself are still very much alive. Their power is just dormant, unable to yield itself in Valley Low's energy field. The soil buried beneath is trying to help the root grow a bud so that it can reveal itself. There was a tiny crack with a tiny twig beginning to sprout where the key lies. I overheard a few Dark Ones talking, and they said that when the key is found, it must be turned in the twisted root tree five times, and only a blueprint has the power to open it."

"Well, we don't want to go during the night," Ostephen said. "That's when the grays really come out."

"But how do we go unnoticed during the day?" Deliah asked.

The crystal wand began to flash. Reaching for it, she saw Merlin. He congratulated her on finding Finvarra, then reminded her of the vile he had given her.

"The golden potion, my dear! The golden vile, and you shall disappear. Wait for the fifth hour tomorrow, the hour of change. The number five will help to transform and rearrange."

They decided that there wasn't nearly enough potion for all of them, so Edwin stayed back because he was so big that it would take all the potion to make him disappear. Kristoff also stayed back because now that the Dark Ones knew he was alive, he would draw too much attention. And so it was settled. Deliah, Ostephen, and Twiglet would drink the golden potion, become invisible to all they should pass, and hopefully find the twisted root key and set Finvarra free. They would embark on this sacred mission tomorrow at the fifth hour.

It may have been daylight, but grays were everywhere. Deliah, Ostephen, and Twiglet rounded a corner quickly and huddled close together. Although the grays couldn't see them, it was important that they not bump into them or call any attention their way. They had made it to within five feet of the tree when Deliah bent down and began searching for a tiny twig or crack. Twiglet knelt down alongside her as Ostephen searched a few feet away. Twiglet poked Deliah's arm and pointed toward what looked like the beginnings of a tiny root breaking through the surface. Ostephen followed their eyes and spotted the mark, and all three smiled and cheered silently.

They had discussed their plan in detail about how they would manage to retrieve the key from underground; surely, this would cause some noise and dust. And, as Kristoff had declared, this would require a distraction of great proportions. This was where he and Edwin would come in.

Ostephen hurried and flew straight up, aware of their limited time with the potion; it would wear off sooner rather than later. He sent a little flash of blue light toward Edwin and his brother—just enough so that Kristoff could see it, but not enough that it would catch a gray's eye. Then in return, and just as they had planned, Ostephen received a sparkle of yellow. They had received the signal. It would be only a matter of minutes before chaos would erupt. They would hopefully have enough time to get the key, free Finvarra, and vanish from Valley Low for good.

They had asked themselves what was the one thing grays couldn't stand? Light. So Kristoff and Edwin set forth a blinding glimmer of rainbow-colored light. Blinded by the light, the grays ducked and wailed. Seeing that the light wasn't fading, the grays all gathered. Cloaked in a circle of darkness, they set out to the top of Valley Low to cover the land in a cloud of gray so that the light couldn't shine through. Edwin and Kristoff were struggling to hold the darkness back when they suddenly heard a familiar voice and turned to see Merlin beside them in a puff of smoke. He pointed his wand in the direction of the grays, and it amplified the rainbow color, sending it into a swirling circle of bright mists, fading into one another. It began to break up the dark cloud, and the grays got angrier and louder, wailing with discontent.

Deliah, Ostephen, and Twiglet rushed to dig and break apart the rock. Determined to widen the gap, Deliah kept thrusting her wand into the cracked, dry land. They saw a root and scrambled to pull it out but were sent flying backward on to their behinds. The wailing of the grays got louder and louder as they drifted closer to the top. They felt panicked for their friends, and Ostephen began chanting "Finvarra, Fin Fin Faye!" over and over. Deliah and Twiglet joined him, and the crystal wand started to glow. She slammed it down into the earth as they all held it and chanted Finvarra's name over and over.

On the fifth chant, the wand glowed a bright white, and the earth began to part. They pulled on the root once more, chanting and sweating. Finally, it broke free and seemed happy to be in Deliah's hands. They all cheered, but their celebration was cut short as they saw their friends' light barely holding up against the grays' cloud overhead.

Deliah heard Merlin's voice in her head: *Hurry, child.*

She ran to the tree, searching for a keyhole. They all looked desperately but couldn't find it.

Twiglet laid his head against the bark and whispered, "Help us."

He leaned his twigs against the tree, and feeling with his arm, he managed to make out a tiny crown etched in the bark, barely visible to the eye.

"Try this! Try this!" he exclaimed.

Deliah placed the three points at the end of the twisted root key into the bark. It fit but was snug.

"Nothing's happening! What now?" she cried.

"Turn it five times, remember?" Ostephen said encouragingly. Using all her strength, Deliah turned it clockwise five times. On the last turn, the key fell to the ground, and the tiny carved crown in the bark glowed gold. The tree slowly rattled and shook before it was suddenly sucked down into the ground, disappearing completely as though it never existed.

"Oh, no! What have we done?"

They all stood forlorn with heads bowed, then they realized that the sky was turning dark. They looked up to see the grays headed their way. They also noticed that the potion had faded, and they were visible and defenseless.

Hearing a sharp whistle, they looked up to find a tall, dark-haired man waving them over. His blue eyes sparkled with love, and without hesitation, they all breathed a sigh of relief.

"Finvarra!" they all said excitedly.

"Indeed," he said, "hurry now. We haven't much time."

Finvarra was tall, dark, and handsome. He was dressed in a suit of burgundy velvet with gold lining. He looked regal. His broad shoulders carried an air of confidence, and his shirt was emblazoned with the symbol of Faye.

The grays were fast approaching now, and they all held their breath, waiting for the attack when a great white light shot down the middle of the grays, and a magnificent unicorn skidded to a halt at their feet.

"Edwin!" they shouted with relief.

Merlin sat atop the unicorn now, casting a beam of white light to try to postpone the grays. They all scrambled onto Edwin's back. Kristoff and Ostephen proudly sat in the king's chest pocket, elbowing each other and smirking at how grand they must look as royalty. Deliah held on to Twiglet who held onto Merlin's cape for dear life. Just as the grays wailed mournfully and charged rapidly, Edwin was gone.

Chapter 17

There is so much love to go around.
There is so much light to be illuminated.
Be the match to ignite the flame,
For soon there will be no igniting left, as only light remains.

S afe and sound back in the forests of Faye, the king fell to the ground and kissed the earth. He stood, eyes filled with tears of joy, and profusely thanked all of them before coming to Deliah. Being very familiar with the prophecy, he bent down on one knee and plucked a smiling flower from beside him and wrapped it around Deliah's pinky finger, making a ring.

"I could not be happier to see the prophecy of Faye being fulfilled, and we have you to thank for it." The tiny pink rose on her finger continued to smile at her. "Too long I have been captured, hidden, and forced to remain silent and asleep."

He stood, and for the first time, Deliah realized how utterly tall and majestic he truly was. They all embraced him and shouted, "Fin Fin Faye!"

Finvarra raised his right hand to his heart and said, "We've traveled far. We've traveled wide. In Faye, we have bestowed our pride. To love, to laugh, to live, to play, may Faye conquer all and see a new day."

As Deliah sat quietly, yawning and fighting off sleep, she couldn't imagine how life could ever be the same. How was she supposed to go home after all the amazing and curious things she had seen and experienced? It was then that her heart gave a little sigh, and she realized that she never had to say goodbye. She was looking forward to seeing Grandma and knew she wanted to return to the cottage, Papa's favorite place. She fell asleep by the fire, but instead of drifting off to her usual sweet dreams, she awoke in a cold sweat, fists clenched and terrified.

Unable to find sleep, King Finvarra was awake as well and handed her a mug of warm berry tea.

"It's the Dark King," he said suddenly. "We're too close now. You can't escape it or push it away. He knows we're coming, and he intends to haunt us with night terrors." Finvarra talked at length of Faye's history and the prophecy before assuring Deliah that he had no intentions of letting Faye and all its glorious inhabitants fall prey to the Dark King.

"One light will always overpower any darkness," Deliah said, repeating Papa's wisdom.

Finvarra looked through the fire into Deliah's eyes, raised his cup to hers, and said, "Indeed, indeed it shall."

After managing to find a few hours of sleep, they all gathered around an elm tree and devised a plan. Merlin, seeing that everything was proceeding well, simply tipped his pointy hat and vanished in a puff of smoke and sparkle.

"Merlin, that wise old sage! Still as mysterious as ever, I see," Finvarra stated as he chuckled. "In preparation of the prophecy, there is a forest we can trek through to sneak silently into the Dark Corner. In fact, I believe that with the right guide we can get within a few hundred yards unnoticed. We can call Trin to guide us."

Trin was a forest fairy with dark black hair and emerald green eyes. She was very familiar with the dark forest, as she chose to call it home. Trin appeared in a sparkle of teal light, the blue-green color enhancing her haunting eyes. She was quiet but very charming, and she immediately took to Deliah, flying into her palm and casually sitting cross-legged. Her green stockings were long and slouchy but matched well with her slouchy green hat and roughly hemmed green dress.

"I always knew this day would come," Trin said softly. "And here it is."

• • •

Trin, short for Trinamier, was happily leading her followers

99

through the dark forest when she stopped abruptly as if frozen in time. Ahead she spied five Kahorgis coming their way. They all slowly tiptoed behind a birch tree, but they rustled a branch and accidentally snapped a twig. The Kahorgis grunted and charged as Trin and the rest tried to huddle closer together and hide. The Kahorgis were searching and sniffing, tearing apart every branch, trying to find the noise makers.

Out of nowhere came a loud, exaggerated weeping sound. The Kahorgis immediately changed direction and followed it, forgetting all about the snapping twig. Deliah breathed a huge sigh of relief and they all peeked around the edge of the birch tree. They could see the Kahorgis grunting and gnashing their teeth at a willow tree.

"Weepin' Willy!" Deliah cried just as Ostephen and Kristoff covered her mouth, trying to stifle the gasp. Removing their hands, she whispered, "How can he be here?"

Ostephen whispered back, "He can uproot himself like any other tree. Weepin' Willy's always been a bit of a wanderer, a sad one at that."

Finvarra remarked on Willy's loyalty, as it was obvious that he had seen his friends in trouble and created a distraction in their favor.

The Kahorgis, fed up with his wailing and unable to decipher any information, wrote him off and trudged onward. Willy slowly lifted a root out of the ground, followed by several more and made his way over to Deliah who moved out from under the birch tree. Deliah embraced Willy at once.

"Thank you!" she said earnestly.

"No pr…prob…problem, ma'am," he sobbed back. Deliah knew that Weepin' Willy was happy to see her even though he seemed unable to show it.

Willy bowed a root before the king and stammered, "Fin… Fin…F…F…Faye!"

The king bowed back. Then standing tall, he told Weepin' Willy that he was an honorable tree who had earned a reward. He explained that as the King of Faye, he could bestow titles.

"If only I had something ceremonial to offer you besides a title," he mused aloud.

Deliah's pocket within her cape began to glow, and she

100

saw that it was the vial of green liquid Merlin had given her. She pulled it out and handed it to Finvarra.

"Merlin gave me this. Perhaps it will do?"

"Ah, certainly," Finvarra said relieved. He took the wooden cork out of the vile and poured it over Willy, declaring "Willy, Willow of Honor and Rightful Protector of Faye."

Deliah was about to clap in excitement when they were all stunned to silence. The green liquid and light from the vile that Willy absorbed had gathered and was now coming out the top of his head and forming a tiny raincloud. Only it wasn't producing rain. It seemed to be sucking tears right out of Willy before it burst with water and then shot up into the sky. There Willy stood, bright-eyed and free. He now spoke smoothly and almost eloquently. Deliah couldn't believe it. He was more vibrant than ever and was smiling from leaf to leaf.

"I'm free!" he shouted. He hugged Deliah and the king, thanking them, although they had no idea what they'd done.

"Try and talk now, Weepin' Willow!" they exclaimed gleefully.

Willy didn't stammer or weep once, and he explained that the day Kristoff was captured by the Dark Ones he had been close by. He could see them trying to turn Kristoff, and he tried to protect Kristoff by yelling at him not to listen to them and to hear his truth. He was distracting Kristoff, and for a while it worked. Then they took Kristoff deeper into the forest where Willy couldn't interfere. The Dark Ones came back later and cast a spell on Willy: the sob spell.

"It was not long after that they finally managed to turn Kristoff, and it seemed all had been lost. I couldn't tell anyone of the spell, or they said it would remain permanent, and I would never be free of it."

Kristoff flew forward, shook a leaf, and said, "Willy, I remember now! I remember you trying to get me to not listen to the Dark Ones in the forest, and I remember ignoring you and following them. I can't tell you how much it means to me that you tried to save me. I'm sorry you have had to suffer. Thank you. I am indebted to you."

"Not at all," Willy replied. "Your friendship is all I need."

Because fairies and peoples of Faye love parties, they decided to celebrate in Willy's honor right then and there. Before parting, Finvarra asked Willy to keep an eye out for Faye and to alert him of any suspicious behavior or unwelcome visitors.

"Most certainly," Willy said with a smile.

Weepin' Willy

Chapter 18

Believe indeed; believe I do,
For when you believe, life unfolds to you.

Half a day later, as they continued through the dark forest, Deliah saw a red glow coming from her bag. Until now, she had all but forgotten about the ruby Dedrik had given her. Upon seeing its ravishing red glow, Kristoff flew over and stood somewhat hypnotized. Ostephen flew over and hovered beside him, waving his hands and snapping his blue fingers in front of Kristoff's face, finally breaking his hypnotic trance. Somewhat embarrassed, Kristoff nodded appreciatively and hovered back a few feet.

The ruby projected a red light into the air, and as if watching a movie unfold before them, they saw the Dark Corner, the Dark King, the Kahorgis, and his other loyal followers. The Kahorgis had apparently grown in number. The picture the ruby reflected was one Deliah didn't care for. They saw the Dark King sitting on his dingy throne. Slightly disarmed at the number of Dark Ones and Kahorgis, Finvarra released a sigh before the picture faded, and he turned to his friends. Ostephen, Deliah, and Kristoff were all holding hands, trying hard to be brave.

"Deliah, walk with me," Finvarra said. Ostephen and Kristoff followed, but Finvarra kindly asked them for privacy. "This needs to be between a — well, just us, you see." They nodded understandingly and went to talk with Edwin and Trin.

Deliah had a million things running through her mind: Are we in trouble? Does he think we'll lose Faye and that we should give in and turn back? Have I messed up somewhere, somehow?

Finvarra stopped, and they each took a seat across from each other on two large rocks.

"I'm not sure how to tell you this, Deliah, but there is only one person who can help us right now."

"Wonderful!" she answered excited. "Who is he?"

"It is the one who is of my blood, one who has the blood of Faye coursing through their very veins. It is the only one who has access to Hallimer's Halls and all the soul prints of Faye."

"Like Faye royalty?"

"Yes, exactly. This is the only being with blood born of the King of Faye, the only soul who has access to the divine records in Hallimer's Halls, the only one who can access the records and call forth whatever souls are needed."

"So we're not outnumbered!" Deliah grasped enthusiastically.

"Right, this person is only entitled because it is written in the prophecy that the only child of Finvarra, King of Faye, shall have access. Only the one in the prophecy. Only she…."

He stared at Deliah intently searching for some kind of recognition, but she appeared lost.

"So there's another? Another girl who is part of the prophecy? Another girl who is half-human, half-elemental?"

"No, there is only one, dear child."

"But, it can't be. It doesn't make any sense. We're not….I'm not….It can't be."

"Deliah, you are of my blood. You have Faye coursing through your very veins."

Deliah held on to the side of her rock, feeling the need to be grounded.

"My father is Sam," she stated.

"I won't deny this. In every way he has been and will forever be your father. Yet you, Deliah, were born in Faye, to Faye, of Faye. Upon my being captured, you were brought to Sam shortly after your arrival by Mayweather and Cordelia. They left you with him to be raised in protection, to be shielded and kept secret from the Dark King.

"Why are you doing this? Why are you saying this?" she asked as she kicked at her rock with both heels.

"Because the time is now. You need to know the truth to fulfill your purpose."

Deliah thought back to times when she had questioned Papa about her mother or other family. He never answered her directly; he just said that he was always alone and that he never knew love until the glorious gift of baby Deliah landed in his life. Because she was so happy with him and felt so loved, she let it go. She felt she had all she needed. The two of them were always enough.

"Deliah, you were born unto Faye in a sparkle of silver light, a shine so bright the stars called you their very own. You are Deliah, Fairy Princess of Faye, daughter of Finvarra and Maeve."

"Maeve? Fairy princess? Maeve is Queen of Faye?"

Deliah's head was spinning. The last time she had felt this confused, she had been lying in the grass before stumbling upon a lot of little people and somehow winding up here!

"Yes, she is a queen by every right and my one true love. It has forever been in the prophecy that the girl who would fulfill it would be deemed our child and would indeed be born half-human blood, half-Faye blood. You see, unlike Maeve, I have incarnated in human form many lifetimes to understand the human realm and their reasons for not seeing us and trusting in Mother Nature. Because of these lifetimes, I am also like you: half-human, half-fairy."

Deliah momentarily lost all sense of time and space, even forgetting about the gravity of the situation. She let herself get lost in a daydream of being a fairy princess—something she had always dreamed of. In the daydream, she was in a beautiful gown and had wings! She was dancing with a very cute fairy prince… very cute….

"Deliah! Deliah! Deliah!"

She heard her name echoing throughout her dream and suddenly snapped back to reality.

"Oh, why wasn't I born one or the other? Why am I not fully fairy or fully human?"

"That is a very good question, my child. It is because of your purpose. You are protected by the prophecy. This is why you are special, Deliah. The Dark King and his servants cannot steal your energy or your soul. You are protected and unique by

106

being born of Faye yet holding the energy of two realms. This is how it must be to fulfill the prophecy. Humans like you who are so deeply connected to Faye and the fairy realm never lose their fairy characteristics or traits. It is innate; we know how to coexist in each realm. Soon all humans will discover that this coexistence is possible and natural. I may suggest that your future holds a bridging of the two worlds. Perhaps if you continue to embrace your truth as well as you have, you may very well be the bridge. I can only dream that one day all humans will come to accept our existence and welcome our help, stop hurting Mother Earth, and learn to live in harmony with all of nature and its creations."

Deliah was staring past Finvarra in a haze of mixed emotions, all the while feeling overwhelmed.

"So, my dear, Maeve will be joyously happy to see you. Immediately after your arrival, I was captured. I sent word with Sidney the squirrel, one of a few nearby who saw me as I was taken. I had Maeve flee Faye to honor the prophecy and to keep her safe as well. Thank God for that squirrel. I have sent word for Maeve's return; she shall arrive back in Faye any day now. Twelve years has been a long time to wait."

Deliah smiled as she saw Finvarra soften at the very thought of her. He sighed and then cleared his throat and got back to business.

"So, Hallimer's Halls. It is a large building full of books, records, and scrolls of all kinds. You must find your way, unseen by any Dark Ones and find the book marked with the seal of Faye. It will have an *F* marked in purple wax. Upon finding this book, you will bring it back to me, and together we are to open it and access the fairies, humans, knights, gods and goddess—the past and present friends who will come forth and join us."

"Like in the rainbow?" she asked.

"Yes, but that was only the start. We will intensify that very energy and even move the moon if that's what it takes to defend Faye! Are you all right? Can you handle this?" he asked tentatively.

Deliah looked at him solemnly before her eyes fell to the rock, and Finvarra prepared himself for her to say "No." With her answer, Faye could forever vanish. He shuddered at the thought.

Deliah stood in front of the rock, locked eyes with her fairy father, and said, "I'm a fairy princess!"

Finvarra laughed and hugged her heartily. He cupped his hands over hers, and they said in unison, "To Hallimer's Halls!"

Chapter 19

She runs like a child on the happiest of days,
The breeze pushing her forward, happy to play.

As Deliah and Finvarra returned, they saw Ostephen and Kristoff in the middle of a flying competition.

"I win!" Ostephen shouted, shaking his blue butt to and fro in victory.

"No, I win!" Kristoff shouted back, flapping his wings sternly.

Edwin decided to settle it for them, saying "I do believe it was a tie."

Kristoff and Ostephen looked at Edwin, then at each other.

"Fine," they reluctantly agreed.

Finvarra cleared his throat and then said, "I think you should all be aware that Deliah has been informed of the remainder of the prophecy and that our next destination will be Hallimer's Halls."

They all gasped in excitement, and for a moment they regarded Deliah not as their old friend but as royalty. They felt it an honor just to be in her presence.

"I'm goin' with ya!" Ostephen said instantly, placing his hands on his tiny hips for emphasis.

"And I'll keep lookout!" added Kristoff, flying up and sitting on Edwin, lifting his little yellow hand to his forehead as a visor, peering to and fro, trying to show off his best "lookout" skills. In that moment, he spotted some pink and red glowing lights coming from below a nearby hill.

"Let's check it out!" he and Ostephen shouted.

They were about to make their way down the hill when they heard a rustle in the bushes and stiffened in fright.

Edwin bowed his head and said, "Do not be worried, my king. I believe this to be a most welcome visitor." He moved to the side, revealing a tall, mahogany-haired fairy draped in a gold gown covered with sparkling pink crystals. She was wearing pointed gold slippers, each with a pink crystal on the toe. Her hair sparkled with tiny pink jewels that glowed alongside her green eyes.

Deliah stared in fascination at the precious pink crystals in her hair and then noticed that they were set in a tiny gold crown.

"The queen!" she muttered under her breath.

At the very same moment, Finvarra shouted, "My love!"

He rushed to her side and knelt, kissing her hand before standing and hugging her close. The queen's eyes welled up with tears of joy; she was truly relieved to see Finvarra safe and sound.

"My dear king, how I've missed you so!"

As Finvarra kissed her, glorious pink butterfly-like wings that reached from head to toe unfolded from Maeve's back. She was so stunning that Deliah was in utter awe. Finvarra clasped Maeve's hand in his, and they walked toward Deliah.

"My sweet princess," Maeve said, looking at Deliah adoringly. "You make me so very proud."

She hugged Deliah, and to her surprise, she didn't feel any hesitation, just complete warmth, love, and joy.

"I'm glad you're back," Deliah said. "Finvarra told me…."

"Yes, it was terribly difficult leaving then, but I had faith that I would see both you and my love again, and so it is."

She smiled while cupping Deliah's face in her hands. A look of true splendor and pride beamed across Maeve's face.

"My love," Finvarra said, "our next stop is Hallimer's Halls to access the book of Faye."

"Yes, I know. Merlin alerted me to your whereabouts. He knew I was anxious to find you. However, before you leave me again," she teased, "the flower fairies have put together a beautiful feast for us. Let us enjoy one another's company for a time before you move on," she said with a voice as soft as the sea.

Finvarra squeezed her hand gently in agreement. The sun had set, and it was just turning dark when they all followed Maeve down a slight hill. At the bottom of the hill, they saw a glowing heart shape made of pink and red dragonfly lights. In the middle of the heart-shaped lights was a feast full of every treat you could ever ask for. There were cupcakes, tarts, chocolate-covered berries, pies, cakes, and every kind of delectable fruit. There were so many treats that you couldn't even see the marvelous mahogany table underneath them. The matching stumps of wonderful wood served as chairs, thirty-three to be exact. There was not a space left open that wasn't covered in sweets or topped with flowers. The flowers included pink and red roses, lilies, peonies, hydrangea, carnations, gerbera daisies, and bountiful baby's breath.

Deliah was so awestruck by the pure splendor of it all that she had almost missed taking in all the guests seated at the table. She felt herself fighting back emotion and tears as she waved hello to Mayweather, Rosella, Willy, Twiglet, Pan, Maury, Herbie and a few of the other gnomes who had rescued her, Laflin, Mrs. McCullum, Cordelia, the frog prince, several bush people, Sidney, Merlin, Green Man, Chief Nimble and more. They all stood as Merlin came forth and took one of Maeve's hands and one of Finvarra's in his.

"The King and Queen of Faye are united together again. Nothing makes me happier, and nothing is more powerful than the wondrous gift of love," Merlin declared.

Finvarra gestured to a seat for Deliah beside him and Maeve. With Merlin, they all sat down, basking in the romantic scene the flower fairies had set for them. There were a few flower fairies still nearby, wanting to be assured that their friends had everything they needed, but they chose to stay back, not liking to be the center of attention. Their quiet manner and shy demeanor was alluring, and each flower fairy wore a hat of the flower they were most fond of. There was one with a rosebud on her head and another with a lily. They were so sweet. Ostephen and Kristoff wasted no time digging in, their cheeks bursting as they continuously stuffed their faces. Finvarra made sure Maeve had her favorites and noticed Merlin and Deliah already deep in conversation. Deliah had gathered more than a few cupcakes in front of her—Grandma had baked them all the time, and they were her favorite. She enjoyed watching Maeve and Finvarra; they seemed unbelievably happy together. The whole table shook as Laflin let loose one of his telltale laughs, and Twiglet jumped onto the table to prove to the frog prince that he was mistaken: twigs *can* dance! This sent the bush people and the gnomes into heaves of laughter, which Twiglet momentarily found upsetting before he himself burst out in glee as well. Pan joyfully provided some soft, subtle music throughout the night.

Merlin informed Deliah that not only was he happy to reunite Meave and Finvarra, but he also needed to give Deliah another tool for battle.

"I know at your last gathering they shared with you the power of controlling your thoughts and how to use your breath and concentration to your advantage. Now that you've had some practice with this, Deliah, you can access a deeper level of healing. I want to teach you the gift of regeneration."

He took her aside and described how still using the other techniques and lessons she'd learned, she could find within herself the ability to heal others. Deliah was a bit overwhelmed but listened closely, trusting Merlin's wisdom and gentle manner of teaching.

"Breathe and call forth that which you desire. Set firm your will, and you can change an outcome," Merlin assured her. Merlin also explained to Deliah that while she had been given some tools along her journey, it was actually the underlying message that proved most meaningful.

"Can you tell me what that is? What have you learned along your journey thus far?" he asked her.

Her chest started pounding, and she was suddenly nervous. She didn't want to embarrass herself in front of Merlin. Then she took a deep breath and thought back to everyone she'd encountered and all her experiences. She was twiddling her thumbs. Then in a sudden moment of clarity, she looked Merlin in the eye and said, "Love is the force." He nodded with his sincere smile and tipped his pointy hat, once again disappearing in a puff of smoke.

It was a truly remarkable evening, but everyone knew that tomorrow they would reach Hallimer's Halls and be that much closer to the Dark Corner.

Spirkle

Chapter 20

Have you lost something?
Check your cloak.
Perhaps it's a fairy playing a joke.

The two white doors seemed to reach to the sky and beyond. Alone, Deliah pushed one open and crept inside. The smell of books old and new filled the air. She marveled at how organized it was, yet how chaotic it appeared. Shelf after shelf was lined with books, scrolls, records, and sacred contracts. She felt like a tiny ant, knowing it would be hard to spot her among these gigantic halls. She began to creep cautiously up and down the various halls, looking for the row marked *Faye* as Finvarra had mentioned.

Aha! She found the correct aisle and ran her fingers over the smooth bindings of the books, breathing in their heady scent. The halls emanated wisdom and power; she was sure that every second spent in Hallimer's Halls was a second of knowledge gained. She found a step stool and on her tiptoes frantically sought the purple book with the wax seal. She pulled a large purple book off the shelf and opened it to check. To her astonishment, she spied a tiny creature inside the book, peeking over the binding, causing her to scream in shock. After a few moments, her echo faded as she stared at the creature. His thumbs and fingers were large and gripped the book's edge tightly. All Deliah could see were these huge brown eyes staring back at her from this tiny, round purple head.

All of a sudden, the creature spoke, "Allo!"

Terrified, Deliah dropped the book and ran to the other side of the aisle. She peered around the corner to see if the book and its inhabitant were still there. There was a sparkle of light as the book closed, but there was no trail of the wide-eyed creature. With her heart slowly finding its regular beat again, she regained her focus and studied the shelves.

"Purple book, where are you?" Deliah mumbled frustrated.

Suddenly, there was a sparkle of white light, and she saw the same creature peering over another book's edge from inside it. She stiffened as it locked its attention on her. It then slowly raised one of his round, long fingertips and pointed to the shelf below her. Another sparkle of white and a wink, and it was gone.

Deliah bent down, counted three books over, and to her bewilderment noted a large purple wax seal with an *F* marked in it. She grabbed it quickly and hugged it tightly to her chest, aware of its precious cargo.

"Thank you," she said humbly, looking around for the wide-eyed creature.

Suddenly, the book fell open, and he popped up once again from inside it, gripping its edges tightly.

"Spirkle," he said in a high-pitched voice. "Spirkle's me name."

He extended a hand, and Deliah reached out and shook his long, slender finger.

"Ask 'em," Spirkle said. "Ask 'em all for help. They all knew you'd be comin'. At least we all hoped! Go on and ask 'em!"

Before Deliah had a chance to open her mouth and say thank you, he vanished once again. She sat cross-legged on the floor and gently ran her hand over the book's smooth cover, sliding a finger down the gold lining, appreciating its beauty. A book fell off a shelf in front of her and opened. Spirkle peered out.

"You gotta ask first! Ask and then you'll see. Just ask and then you'll see...."

Deliah was starting to wish Spirkle might stick around a bit longer, so she could ask him some questions, but he seemed to be adept at disappearing. She held the edges of the book of Faye—the seal still intact—and closed her eyes.

"Please help me. Please help us. Please help Faye."

She opened her eyes and was stunned to silence as she saw the halls packed from ceiling to floor with souls, thousands of them all hovering in the air. They were of all ages and sizes: some children, an older gentleman smoking a pipe, several knights in armor, gods, goddesses, wizards, scientists, all creatures and animals past, and so many more. She was quite taken aback but not at all scared.

She hugged the book to her chest and slowly stood. No one was talking, and she thought, *So this is what an uncomfortable silence must feel like!*

They all laughed appreciatively, and she realized she may have said that aloud, or they were telepathic as Merlin had mentioned.

"Um, thank you," she said shyly.

A knight stepped forward and bowed before her.

"No, thank you," he said. "Let the king know we are all ready and awaiting his call."

Deliah smiled, and all the souls nodded in recognition. Her heart warmed, and for the first time since she had used the ruby and caught a glimpse into the Dark Corner and its army, she felt as though they might actually stand a chance.

Deliah knew she'd be allowed entrance to Hallimer's Halls, but she never gave thought to the trouble she'd have getting out. She looked out the windows and saw Dark Ones and Kahorgis around every corner wall. She knew her friends were out there, but she had no idea how she was to go about getting to them. What if the Dark Ones had snuck up and captured them? She knelt in a corner well hidden from the windows and prayed for help.

She was obviously in the right place because instantly a group of twenty or more souls appeared floating before her and said, "Your friends have created a diversion on the east side. You are to exit there, and all will be well."

She bowed her head in thanks. They guided her to the proper door and wished her well.

"When the book is opened, you will see us all again," they said.

Just then Deliah swore she heard her name. Maybe it was just a bee buzzing by? Or maybe it was…Ostephen! He had managed to sneak in through a crack, and he whispered the plan of escape to Deliah. The souls, still nearby, listened and offered their help.

They all took a deep breath, and Ostephen quickly darted out the door, buzzing left then right, up then down, confusing several Dark Ones. Annoyed, they let him go and focused on the door, waiting for Deliah and the book. The souls enveloped Deliah in the center and momentarily blinded the Dark Ones with their white light and power. The Dark Ones screeched in pain and frustration, giving Deliah enough time to run safely back to the trail to meet her friends. The souls knew that the Dark Ones could never gain access to the halls because the energy of Hallimer's Halls simply wouldn't allow it.

Now in the safety of her friends, Deliah thought that Hallimer's Halls seemed almost too easy. She found it comforting to know that they would have the support of all those souls from all the records and scrolls, but she started to wonder if it wasn't all just an illusion. She realized there was no end to the magic and surprises that existed in Faye. Many times she was frightened, yet somewhere deep within her there was an innate sense of comfort, of safety, of déjà vu. It was like she knew she was in the right place at the right time. After all, she seemed to keep getting clue after clue, meeting each and every person she needed along the way. It just seemed so fateful.

• • •

Deliah ran to Finvarra, still tightly gripping the book of Faye. She paused, so filled with excitement that she was at a loss for words. She held out the book, and Finvarra hugged her, smiling proudly.

"Well done, my dear, well done! Now that we have the book, we have the souls and therefore all we need. We shall prepare for the Dark King. Follow my lead."

He led Deliah and all her friends to the enchanted castle of Faye where he and Maeve resided. It was an unbelievably beautiful elm tree that contained furniture carved of wood. Pictures taken in fairy dust decorated the walls, and it was filled with all the warmth and love of Faye.

As they sat by the fire still holding the closed book of Faye, Deliah truly felt as though they were a happy family. Maeve and

Finvarra were chatting happily. Ostephen and Kristoff, whom she'd come to see as her brothers, sat close playfully teasing one another and her. Her heart swelled with a fullness she hadn't felt before.

As she let her big eyes wander through the enchanted castle, she thought, *If anything could conquer evil, it would be this feeling, this magic.*

"Bam!"

Deliah sneezed and coughed from the sudden impact of a cloud of fairy dust over her head. She looked over and saw Ostephen's sorry glance.

"That was intended for Kristoff," Ostephen explained, pointing to his yellow brother who was mocking his terrible aim. Deliah sneezed again, and a cloud of glitter exploded from her nose and around her face. There was a moment of silence before they all broke out in hysterical laughter, rolling on the ground with glee.

After they were all seated again, Deliah remembered she had a question to ask Maeve—one that had been on her mind ever since her fairy princess awakening.

"In Pan's omen about the prophecy, he mentioned the girl having wings. Is there any chance I could ever have wings?"

Maeve looked at her with gentle eyes, and Deliah began to blush, embarrassed. Maeve leaned forward and whispered, "You already do."

"Your wings unfold when they are ready. They're like fruit," Ostephen said enthusiastically. "They need to ripen before they unfold."

Maeve nodded and said, "Soon enough, sweetie. When they do unfold, it's important that you control them. They can be seen or unseen as will be necessary in your realm."

Deliah was quiet, and they all assumed she was absorbing the news, but she was silently willing her wings to grow a wee bit quicker.

They all enjoyed some tea and then settled in for the evening. Finvarra found a quiet spot with Deliah, and together they opened the book to call on the souls. They pulled back the purple cover, and a golden glow shot out of the book, filling the night sky like a huge hologram. Deliah recognized some of the souls from the hall. Finvarra seemed slightly relieved at the number of souls and help.

A knight stepped forward and spoke, "I see it is time, my king. We will follow you into battle wherever you lead us. We are loyal to Faye—past, present, and future. You have our full allegiance."

"I could not ask for anything more. Your loyalty is deeply appreciated, and your honor is beyond admirable. I thank you," Finvarra responded before filling them in on where the battle would commence. "After we reach the Dark Corner, there is no turning back. They are waiting for us there. Come dawn," Finvarra warned, "the battle will begin."

The souls all knelt before Finvarra and assured him that they would be ready. He could close the book now. They needn't be called upon again; they were his.

Chapter 21

An open heart shall be the key
To seeing that which you wish to see.

Upon awakening the next morning, the air felt different in the castle—and everywhere else for that matter. Every woodland creature and resident of Faye had received word that today they would rise against the Dark King and his castle. It wasn't worry or fear, but there was an intense suspense that gripped the entire realm. The reality of the day had at last hit home.

As they all left the enchanted castle, they joined hands and walked through the rest of Faye to the Dark Corner. One by one, Faye's friends and inhabitants joined the group. Tree after tree uprooted itself, birds flew in flocks larger than anyone had ever seen, and every critter far and wide scurried to join the rallied force.

As they came to the edge of Faye, it was as if they were sitting on the brink of two worlds. Behind them, the sun shone as the clouds sparkled in the clear blue sky. In front of them was nothing but black sky and crashing lightning. From the dark mist surrounding the dark land, a blood red hue seeped through the air as the army of Dark Ones and Kahorgis emerged. The Dark King stepped forward and unfolded his long, black, wicked wings as he signaled for his minions to stop. The sky sparkled as all the fairies and creatures of Faye moved closer until King Finvarra, standing tall in front, signaled them to stop. Finvarra displayed his distinguished, dragonfly-like wings before wrapping them around his chest.

The Dark Lord bellowed at Finvarra and demanded, "Give me the girl!"

Finvarra's wings flared out again as he soared into the air, shouting back "The light prevails today!"

He flew back to his troops of elementals. The Dark King stood, staring at Finvarra and the elementals, watching their auras expand, radiant and luminous.

He shouted, "Fools! All of you!" and dashed back to his minions.

The Kahorgis ran and charged toward the elementals as the Dark Ones took to the sky to attack from above. The sky was now a muddled, murky gray; it was a mixture of pulsating auras of color from Faye and blood red black from the Dark Corner.

Finvarra pulled out the golden sword of Faye and raised it to the sky as the fairies of Faye fluttered into the air to head off the Dark Ones. The Kahorgis leapt into the elementals, clawing and shredding the auras and beams of light they were casting.

"The light will prevail!" Finvarra shouted as he began to charge his enemy.

One of the male dragons glided over, looked at Deliah and then at Ostephen, and said, "Protect her with your life."

He then jetted into the air, his eyes gleaming red. Red heat and flame could be seen in his mouth as he dove down toward the battle and flew across the middle of the Dark King's army, incinerating them in fire, Kahorgis and Dark Ones falling to ash. The Dark King rose and shot bolts of lightning and bursts of flame toward him, hitting his left wing and causing him to fall to the ground badly hurt, unable to move. Dedrik saw the Dark King standing over one of her dragons; she breathed fire as she batted her golden lashes, and she glided toward the Dark King who immediately shot into the air. Continuing to swoop by the injured dragon in pursuit of the Dark King, Dedrik hurled a stream of fire, burning and singeing the Dark King's wings. Several Dark Ones attacked, and Kahorgis leapt from the ground in defense of their king, but Dedrik landed and tossed them aside with her talons.

Kristoff charged forward on top of Edwin, whose silky white

mane blew in the breeze. There was a horrible burning smell and ashes now covered the formerly green ground. Ostephen and Kristoff turned around to see who could possibly be laughing during this ordeal and found Laflin standing over a Dark One, his gold coins rattling away in his pocket.

His wife was nearby and yelled out, "Finally met a match yer own size. Yer a big man now aye, honey?"

Fireballs were thrown left and right, met by splashes of color, sparkle, and blinding white light. The dark gray wind howled deep into the dark, swirling and encompassing all it touched in a cloud of fear and doom. Merlin raised his hand and held his staff out horizontally before him. The wind faded to a mere whistle and was gone. A melody of soft serene notes took its place.

Finvarra knew that to ultimately defeat the Dark King and rid the earth of the Dark Corner, his sword, the golden sword of Faye, had to be thrust into the Dark King's throne by both the King of Faye and the child of the prophecy. Seeing that Dedrik had the Dark King cornered, Finvarra and Deliah snuck away and momentarily left the battle to the rest of their friends as they descended upon the Dark Castle. The souls of Hallimer's Halls had gathered around Deliah and Finvarra, creating a shield of protection. With their help, Deliah and Finvarra managed to sneak inside, escaping all the remaining Dark Ones and Kahorgis on the battlefield.

Inside, the souls all stood guard around Deliah and Finvarra. They slowly approached the ragged, dirty monstrosity of a throne and walked up the two disheveled steps to it. Finvarra nodded ever so slightly, gripped the handle of the golden sword between both fists, and drove it into the seat of the dark and dreary throne. Being close to the throne weakened any who were in its presence while it strengthened the Dark King. They could actually feel all the anger, hatred, and fear that had been created and directed upon the lands from this very seat. As Deliah and Finvarra grew even weaker, their eyes slowly started to close, so Finvarra placed his left hand on the sword and looked to Deliah to complete the task.

This was it! This was what they'd been waiting for! Deliah reached out her hand to take hold of the sword and screamed as a large burn formed on the top of her hand. A large, red-hot ember ate away at her flesh. She drew back and writhed in agony. Finvarra ducked as a swarm of Dark Ones buzzed around them, a cascade of large embers falling everywhere. He ran to cover Deliah as the souls surrounded the throne and protected the sword.

Deliah held her hand, wincing at the sting of the raw, burnt flesh; it seemed so deep that she wondered if she could finish this. The Dark Ones buzzed louder, forming an X across the throne, taunting and teasing their enemies. Finvarra instructed Deliah to sit against the wall and not move as he strode fearlessly toward the Dark Ones.

Under his breath he said, "The time has come for Faye to heal, and with this, I invoke the shield. The sun, the moon, the stars are one. The dawn of Faye has just begun!"

The Dark Ones, surprised at his willingness to attack even though outnumbered, threw fireballs toward him. They were even more surprised when the fireballs could not penetrate the golden glow shining forth from Finvarra but instead fell to the ground frozen. Unsure of what to do, the Dark Ones started to retreat. They looked around for Kahorgis for reinforcement but didn't see any. They hissed and sparked, but the look in Finvarra's eyes warned that he would not stand down. It was more than determination; it was a good man in touch with his absolute power.

Still retreating against this "mad king," they were blinded to the little blue fairy that had managed to creep in to tend to Deliah. Ostephen swaddled her hand in some cloth he had found nearby, dropped sparkles of blue on to it, and whispered, "Sparkle and shine just like new, intended to heal by the blue." This instantly made her feel better.

After a few moments, Ostephen said, "Finvarra has invoked the golden light of protection, so go! Go to the throne! I'll decoy the Dark Ones."

Deliah stood and waited for the brave blue fairy to steal the Dark Ones' attention. He flew over and mocked them, leaving bright flashing trails of blue sparkle behind him. The Dark Ones threw flames at his sparkle and started to chase him, but Ostephen could fly faster. He led the dim-witted Dark Ones to the castle door and back on to the battlefield.

Finvarra and Deliah, both glowing golden, stood on each

side of the throne. Without a word, they looked at each other and placed their hands on the hilt of the sword at the same time. They closed their eyes and said, "And here we are, and so it is."

A crack began to form around the sword, which split the throne down the middle, sending it crashing to the ground in two disheveled pieces. The sword lay on the ground, and Finvarra placed it appreciatively back into its holster. The ceiling began to crumble, and large pieces of stone, debris, and dust filled the air. Ducking with their hands above their heads to avoid being hit, Finvarra and Deliah raced for the castle door as it crumbled and crashed around them. They tripped on some debris as they ran out and fell to the ground, scrambling to get as far away from the castle as possible.

As Deliah and Finvarra thrust the sword into the throne, Dedrik breathed a tumultuous flame of fire engulfing the Dark King's entire body. He tried to shield himself, but he had lost his power at the throne's destruction. Unwilling to give up without a fight, he raised his hands to the sky and drew in a thunderous black cloud of doom and murk. Deliah and all of Faye responded by lifting their hands, letting the sunshine, rainbow, and sparkling beauty rise to stand against the Dark King's cloud. The sky was half-light, half-dark. Good versus evil, light versus darkness was upon them. This was the final hour. This was the future of Faye.

A trail of doves that Merlin had gathered at Rainbow's Pass flew into the darkness, disappearing into the treacherous sky. Slowly, they would emerge over and over again with a soul that had been captured, giving it back its freedom, placing it in the care of Faye, and letting it regain its rightful place.

The Dark King's body turned to ash, and in a final rage of flying rock and smoke, all that was left of his shadowy figure emerged in a raging bellow of despair and defeat. His black, smoky figure loomed above his beloved, crumbled castle.

"Fools, this was only the beginning! This was only the beginning!" the Dark King raged as all of Faye sent their energy toward him.

Dedrik and the rest of the dragons flew over, and upon Dedrik's glittered wink, they all breathed one last flame of fire. All that was left of the king, his castle, and his followers was burned to soot. It all burst into the air, disappearing into the Dark Corner as if it never even existed.

After a long pause, everyone gathered together and bowed to Deliah, including Finvarra and Maeve, who wrapped their arms around her and hugged her with pride. She looked to the earth embarrassed and then bowed alongside them all. Perhaps they were all really bowing for Mother Earth. Everyone was thanking her, jumping, and cheering for their freedom. Some shed tears of joy; some jumped and played in glee. It was the largest of any fairy party by far.

"You're the best friend we've ever had," several of her closest friends said.

"We're not friends," Deliah replied. "We're family."

She noticed the male dragon still lying hurt and motionless. She ran to his side. Suddenly inspired, she remembered the tool of regeneration and healing that Merlin had taught her. She closed her eyes and placed her hands on the dragon's body while the rest of the elementals held hands in prayer. She focused all her energy on seeing the dragon healed and alive again.

"I know you can do it. I know you can. Just breathe," she whispered over and over to him.

She felt the dragon's heartbeat pick up pace and his body temperature rise. She opened her eyes and saw that the blood on his wing had disappeared. She stepped back as he slowly lifted his right wing and then his left, rising to his taloned feet. He bowed his head and nuzzled the side of her head in thanks. Deliah wiped away a tear from her cheek, happy to see him alive and so proud that she had learned to trust herself enough to try.

Faye was brighter than ever before. It was as it should be—a magical, majestic utopia. The sun smiled upon Faye that day. Every creature far and wide from earthworms to birds frolicked happily. Mother Earth was again at peace; all was set right; and from that day forward, anyone who had the pleasure of discovering Faye would witness the eternal truth: *If you believe, magic you'll receive.*

Slowly, the dark sky began to part, and Deliah's eyes followed the crack of sunlight that sparkled on the ground. She saw a man walking toward her. Her Papa! She ran to embrace him, and he picked her up and twirled her around in the air. Her mind flashed back to all the wonderful memories of their life together. She knew this moment wouldn't last; she knew that this was a chance to say goodbye given to her by the elementals, maybe like a reward but more like a miracle.

"I love you, Deliah. You have made me the proudest father in the world! You did it! You did it!"

"I love you, Papa. I love you more than anything!"

The black sky had completely dissipated, and Faye shined brighter than ever. Papa blew her a final kiss before heading back home to the sun and sky. Deliah was crying tears of joy, smiling, and rejoicing. The truth rang through the sky and the lands. Forever more, the prophecy had been fulfilled. Faye could now live *happily ever after*.

A short while later….

Chapter 22

Love is here; love is there.
Love is ever present, everywhere.

Deliah's grandmother awoke yawning and feeling more rejuvenated and refreshed than she had in years. Deliah sat on her lap in Papa's favorite chair and asked Grandma if she'd like to hear a story: a story of a little girl who discovered a whole new world, a magical life just waiting to be explored. Her grandmother listened intently, amazed by her granddaughter's imagination.

When Deliah finished the story, her grandmother asked her if she thought such a glorious place as in her tale truly existed.

"Sure, Grandma, right outside the front door."

Grandma laughed, hugging Deliah as she looked at the red, purple, and orange glowing fairies waving hello from outside the window.

"Well, my dear, what shall we do today?" Grandma asked.

"Bake cupcakes and make a crown of dandelions!" Deliah shouted.

"Sounds like some of your favorite things, but it hasn't been that long since we last did them. Don't you want to do something different?"

"Uh-uh," she said, shaking her head hastily. "It feels like forever!"

"Okay then!" Grandma said as she dug in the drawer and pulled out their aprons, handing Deliah hers. "Let's get baking, and then we can enjoy our cupcakes outside while we make our dandelion crowns."

After dinner, Grandma tucked Deliah into bed, and as Deliah surrendered to a final yawn, she could swear she saw Ostephen hovering outside her bedroom window. She threw off her covers, ran to the open window, and saw him holding a tiny suitcase.

"Didn't think I'd leave without sayin' goodbye, did ya?" he teased.

"Where are you going?" she asked, frowning.

"A good friend once recommended that I take a special someone on a long-awaited trip."

Just then, Rosella flew forward, took Ostephen's outstretched hand, and kissed him tenderly on the cheek. Deliah's heart warmed at the very sight of them.

"I'm so happy for you both!" Deliah exclaimed.

"I'll see ya in a few weeks," Ostephen promised. "Until then, try and stay out of trouble, will ya?" he said with a wink.

They all laughed, and she watched Rosella and Ostephen float toward the mammoth moon, all the stars bending to wave hello as they passed. Deliah crawled back into the familiar warmth of her bed, kissed Papa's picture goodnight, and wished all the fairies a safe flight. She closed her eyes, planning to dream of Cordelia's garden party, which she was going to attend tomorrow.

Deliah tossed and turned in the bed, feeling as though she were lying on something. She got up, turned on her bedside lamp, and felt around the covers but didn't spot anything. Turning, she caught a sparkle out of the corner of her eye. Running to the mirror, she gasped in gratitude. Wings! She turned slowly like a tiny doll in a music box, finally feeling like the fairy princess Finvarra had told her she was.

"Deliah?" Grandma asked, opening the door abruptly. "What's the matter, honey? Can't sleep?"

Deliah was frozen. She could still see her wings in the mirror, but she was in full view of her grandmother, and her grandmother didn't seem to notice a thing! She remembered Maeve saying that the wings could go unnoticed in her realm if need be. Deliah smiled and hopped back into bed.

"I think I'm going to sleep really good now, Grandma." Grandma tucked Deliah in once more and kissed her forehead while turning out the light.

"Sleep tight," Grandma whispered and closed the door.
"As the fairies take flight," Deliah heard Papa whisper.

And so our tale has come to an end.
The little girl's heart certainly did mend
With the help of love and some wondrous friends.
Something tells me there's more to come.
After all, a fairy princess has been awakened
And will be in need of some fun....

CPSIA information can be obtained at www.ICGtesting.com
Printed in the USA
LVOW082035220112

265049LV00001B/4/P